This edition brings back into print a novel of decadence, in the tradition of Huysmans, by a famous American playwright. Originally published in a limited edition in 1924 and sold by subscription, it is the sequel to Fantazius Mallare, *suppressed two years earlier by the Federal Government as obscene.*

The Kingdom of Evil *continues the journal of the mad recluse Mallare, who has decided to live beyond reality, now an empty, repugnant memory. It is Mallare's desire to find a world in which he belongs, and out of his madness he creates the monstrous Kingdom of hallucination: "Luminous and strange, its roofs careening like wing-stretched bats it lay encircled by hills—a Satanic toy, a thing of unearthly marvels. Its painted streets beckoned to Mallare. Its demons, horrors and lusts waited for him . . ."*

THE KINGDOM OF EVIL

THE KINGDOM OF EVIL

A Continuation of the Journal of
FANTAZIUS MALLARE

By
BEN HECHT

Twelve Full Page Illustrations by
ANTHONY ANGAROLA

A Harvest/HBJ Book
Harcourt Brace Jovanovich
New York and London

Library of Congress Cataloging in Publication Data

Hecht, Ben, 1893–1964.
The kingdom of evil.

(A Harvest/HBJ book)
Reprint of the ed. published by P. Covici, Chicago.
I. Title.
[PZ3.H355Ki   1978]   [PS3515.E18]   813'.5'2   78-7288
ISBN 0-15-647123-X

First Harvest/HBJ edition 1978

A B C D E F G H I J

THE KINGDOM OF EVIL

The Kingdom of Evil

{1}

Many years passed. Hidden in a room on the river front Fantazius Mallare became a myth to his friends. Those who had known him continued to speak of his strange genius. They remembered the crazed statues he had carved and the venemous paintings he had made. But these, too, disappeared and like Mallare they became myths.

The secret of Mallare's vanishing is contained in his *Journal*. Nothing is known of him during the seven years but what he has written. One can imagine the mystery of his presence among the people of the river front—a gaunt and automatic man. . .

It is no longer possible to determine in reading the *Journal* of Mallare which parts of it are a record of reality and which are the history of the phantoms that, erupting in his brain, obscured an inhospitable world to his senses. Real or mad the adventures of Mallare during these seven years fill his *Journal* with figures and scenes unknown to life. It was Mallare's desire to find a world into which he fitted. And out of this desire he created the monstrous and humorous land he calls the Kingdom of Evil.

Here in this land reality became for him an empty and repugnant memory. But, as he wrote in a former part of his *Journal,* he was too clever to go mad. His brain was too facile to content itself with the distorted flashes of illusion and the babblings of unedited mania.

Reading the cacophonic pages which form a prologue to his strange history of the Kingdom, the process of his journey grows plain. If he must live beyond life, if his soul, nauseated by the consciousness of its humanity, must lift itself out of its prison, his genius was still able to rear the debris of hallucinations into a perfect and astounding architecture. And, as the *Journal* unfolds, it grows obvious, too, that within this world he created out of his madness,

[2]

Mallare, almost to the end, remained sane; remained able to decorate the phantom scene to which he had given himself with logic and splendors.

That Mallare lived in the Kingdom as if it were real, that he suffered and exulted at the foot of its diabolic throne, the pages of his *Journal* testify. He gave his senses to a macabre and preposterous dream, painting on his mind as he had once painted on canvas scenes in which his madness found a sinister embrace. In this Kingdom he describes, he lived as he preferred. Each day the dawn, like a slow flight of silver-winged birds, arose and spread itself over an inner world. Under its phantom sun the Kingdom revealed itself. It lay in the valley as unreal as the horns of Satan. Its towers rose like plumes of many colored smokes. Its streets were alive with an incredible holiday. Its windows glittered like the eyes of innumerable dragons. A strange merriment filled its sky. Wild laughter came from its doors. Luminous and strange, its roofs careening like wing-stretched bats it lay encircled by hills—a Satanic toy, a thing of unearthly marvels. Its painted streets beckoned to Mallare. Its demons, horrors and lusts waited for him like a dark carnival that consumed his madness and through which he moved forever smiling and precise. . .

Toward the end as the Kingdom of Evil begins its disintegration, Mallare's *Journal* reveals for the first time his terror; not of the diabolic mirage but of the world into which he was slipping again. His words like frantic incantations seek to postpone the debacle overtaking his Kingdom. But his dream no longer feeds on his madness. It begins to grow dim.

Whether the strange denouncement he records is real or whether it too is part of the Kingdom is difficult to tell. It seems probable that Mallare, sensing the collapse of this inner world in which he revelled, sought to continue the fantasy by supplying it with flesh and blood; that he struggled for a time against the dissolution of his dream by translating it into a clumsy and even more frightful reality.

But all this is conjecture. There is nothing known but what Mallare himself has written.

[2]

The history of Mallare's flight into the Kingdom of Evil begins with a succession of disordered pages in his *Journal*. It is obvious in their reading that his madness was searching for an escape; that his brain was busy supplying its fever with a dream in which it might expend itself.

There is no reference to the past. A highly developed verbigeration marks the paragraphs. Ideas make futile and stereotyped circles as if language had grown foreign to them. Lucid sentences appear at intervals. He writes suddenly that he lives above a river and that from his window he watches the river twisting like a soiled peacock feather beneath many bridges. Occasionally he reverts to his hatred of life— the sinister maladjustment that was slowly depriving him of consciousness and inspiring his genius to create a dark dream in which he might hide, as he had hidden once before.

"It is impossible to be alone and apart," he writes in his *Journal*, "I close windows and lock doors and still life stands before me like a repulsive phantom not to be denied. The rouged and ponderous tumult of man continues an unbearable murmur in my ears. The futile churn of humanity through the day haunts my thought like an ugly incident. Madness is the only relief from the specter of life; madness in which I may forget that I am a man, forget the little verminous parade over the dung-heap of which I remain a part."

Then, following chapters of incoherence, words end and drawings fill the pages; sketches of curious-shaped windows, apocraphyl beasts, telescopic towers, serpentine designs that formalize into strange temples; a bizarre and tortured ornamentalization growing continually wilder until the unraveling lines become a demoniac pattern, sinister and illegible.

Abruptly after these pages of drawing the history of the Kingdom of Evil begins. There are no longer voiceless sentences. But precisely, cautiously, the dark dream that offered its refuge to Mallare unfolds. The story opens. . .

[3]

From the Journal of Mallare:—

The fog drifted into the city like a great blind moth. It fluttered in the air peering in at high windows. Slowly it stretched its vast wings destroying steeples and rooftops. For a number of hours the fog remained like that.

Behind the fog the city lay, a tangle of silhouettes. The buildings floated in the mists, moving faintly like dark bubbles in the air. Grey and grimacing the city persisted.

It was morning, but from my window I watched the lights go on behind other windows. This made it seem as if night had come, a thick and unnatural night—a night I have sometimes seen in my dreams when I fell asleep after cruel and disordered days.

I left my room and went into the streets. Figures moved grotesquely in the mist. One could not see their faces. They moved without heads, without arms, without legs—their monotonous bodies mutilated into strange and pleasing shapes by the fog.

At noon the fog became heavier. The great moth hovered closer and closer to the ground. Broken ribbons of mist arose from the sidewalks and fluttered like a new and mysterious race at the heels of the crowd. Spirit figures striking cataleptic attitudes, attenuated and monstrous companions, began to embrace the crowd. I watched these until they, too, disappeared.

An odor like the odor of an old sea wind lay in the air. An invisible rain soaked the streets. The ghost of a lost sea was prowling the day. Immense clouds began to belly their way through the thoroughfares. Gigantic parasols opened over the pavements. An incredible flora ballooned through the city, taking shape out of the thick white mist. Leaf-like walls bloomed over the heads of the crowd. Opaque and spectral flowers soared out of the air. Vast and bulbous, the fungus shapes fashioned themselves into elephantine trees and petals. Behind them the buildings became a vague tracery of pencil lines. Slowly the pencil lines vanished. There were no longer buildings.

The fog was removing the city, obliterating inch by inch the low-ceilinged streets in which the crowd continued moving. Above their heads the office windows flickered for a time like fireflies seen in some occult night and then went out. The store fronts, blazing with electricity, ate yellow edges into the fog. These also vanished. The last things to disappear were the headlights of the traffic that, surrounding itself with noises of alarm, continued to creep invisibly through the mist.

The city became then like an island in space; an island without sky or contours. The people grew frightened. I could see none of them but their presence persisted. Within the blankness that had fallen they were still moving, still groping their ways in pursuit of their little greeds.

But the terror was beginning. Invisible doorways were emptying invisible hosts into the empty panorama of fog. Shouts, screams, clanging of bells and whistlings increased. A din, muffled and monotonous like the wailing of a paralyzed monster poured tremulously out of nowhere. Hidden from each other, their world erased from their smug little eyes, the people slowly came to a halt. Movement stopped. Searchlights vainly discolored the mist. Cries of panic, shouts of horror trembled like little matches of sound and then expired. . .

Gone—all of it—the identity of life. A mist implacable as oblivion, yielding neither to lights nor sounds; a monster of space, a thing without size or content had consumed the world. Gorged, motionless, it lay upon the streets sucking into its depths all that had been.

In vain the little people clutching each other lasciviously, whispering in horror, laughing suddenly and foolishly at the thought of tomorrow, struggled in the invisible bowels of this white death. . .

I write now when nothing can be seen. I still feel the paper under my hand. But there is nothing. Outside my window—nothing. There is no window, no world. Lost within the white phantom of fog the people moan, shudder and wait. The mist like a dream obliterates them, creeps into them and erases their senses. They go mad. They throw their arms about one another. They collapse in great heaps, legs intertwined, faces pressing upon one another in desperate and invisible kisses.

I can see nothing. But there are still sounds. I would like for a moment to have eyes for the strange thing in the fog; for the little heaps of bodies tangled in each other like rain-choked worms; for the glimpses of finger-spread hands clawing at the empty monster. All this life that flowed so proudly through streets and buildings —the blind moth comes and brushes it away with feather wings. An odor remains.

Where are monuments and structures now, the ingenious toys, the eternal and verminous parade? Let it end this way. How white and simple it becomes. A virginal silence. The odor lingers. It too will pass. The white moth alone will remain. . .

[4]

From the Journal of Mallare:—

He is a gigantic man with a large head. His face is expressionless. When he looks at me he seems made of wax. Yet he is stronger than a hundred men. A hundred, I write! There is no limit to his strength. The three hundred of us on this island are paper bags in his hands.

When I have talked to him it has seemed to me that even the stone hills that surround us would split and fall away, if not under his fists then under his voice or his eyes. He is a monster, waxen and invulnerable, or we would have slain him long ago.

In the vast caves **under the hills we** do nothing but discuss his murder. Our leaders continue to address us. I listen calmly. Futility is always amusing. And these little ones in the caves are so righteous and outraged and so frightened. A great wrong has been done them. They have been stolen from the world. And, overcome with fear of their predicament, they boast desperately to one another how indispensable they were. There will be a great search for them.

An old man rises. He is bald and wears a beard which makes his head look upside down. But his little watery eyes command attention. His clothes are torn and soiled. His withered, stringy body is exposed. He looks, as he stretches out his hand for our attention, like a senile and pedantic Robinson Crusoe. He talks slowly and with a patriarchal anger. He repeats what we have already heard a hundred times and to me, at least, the repetition is beginning to seem ridiculous.

He announces who we are. As he talks I amuse myself thinking of the unprecedented shock in his mind. A short while ago he was Professor Jacobi, a famed and aged man still playing like a fanatic child in his laboratory. He wore a skull cap and occasionally addressed an auditorium filled with dignified and obsequious colleagues. The world paused now and then in its Saturnalia of greed to turn its ears to his voice—a voice that promised calmly and authoritatively that new secrets were being wrested from

nature; that science was fashioning new toys out
of life.

Now this venerable magician stands in rags,
his little eyes blinking and watering and his
brain, snatched from its dreams and obsessions,
rattling angrily behind its words. We are the
great ones of the world, he says, and our kidnaping is not so much a personal outrage as a crime
against humanity. Ah, how comforting this fact
remains to us, helpless and terrified in our cave.
I look at my fellow captives and the humor of
the situation overcomes me. Here is a jest at
which one may laugh with all one's senses. What
a thundering and ridiculous crew we are. The
great ones! A rabble of savants—dreamers,
builders, artists, inventors, investigators, organ-
izers, scientists. A collection of monomaniacs
whom the world proudly identified a short time
ago as its leaders of medicine, its wizards of
chemistry; its internationally famous astrono-
mers, engineers, architects, physicists, poets,
painters, paleontologists, psychiatrists, philoso-
phers. No profession is missing. Here we all
are—the high priests of progress, the immemor-
ial horses of genius dragging the race inch by

inch out of the infinite dark which gave it birth.

Jacobi continues. Why do we sit like this, like impotent children thrust away in a labyrinth of caves? What will become of our experiments, inventions; of our half-conquered secrets?

Another rises, venerable and expansive. He has taken with him out of the world a secret indispensable to mankind, he assures us for the tenth time, an alloy to displace steel and stone and revolutionize the face of the earth. He is Callavaro, the atomic investigator, and we listen with attention. Another few months and his experiments would have been completed. Now here he stands, his formulae useless, his great work dying emptily in his head. It is imperative that something be done quickly.

One by one they rise and talk, each babbling of his interrupted researches, of the gap left behind. It has become a congress of frustrated saviors. I notice that some of the listeners smile. Bernhard the philosopher strokes his beard, his eyes twinkling. Jensen the engineer, inquires persistently for something to smoke although the tobacco gave out a week ago, and his broad face seems mysteriously elated. The jest is beginning

to receive a reluctant applause. Nevertheless a
new speaker rises. He is more familiar to us than
the others—at least more familiar to me.

He is General Piltendorff, who a few years
ago waged war against the world. Bull-necked,
powerful-jawed, age has not fouled the symmetry
and vigor of his body. He is almost a giant. A
stubble of beard has grown on his face and his
clothes, hanging in tatters, testify to his tireless
activity during the days. He has explored the
caves, climbed like an ape over their rock
shelves, pried into their fantastic crevices—
reconnoitering and searching. Now his body
bleeding from scratches, his bruised feet uncovered, his heavy fists clenched, he stands like some
unbroken savage and hurls angry words at us.
Behind his words one can feel his crude and
powerful mind refusing itself with blows and
oaths to the idea of captivity.

He startles his listeners. Will they who
profess themselves great and superior sit like
this; like white mice in a cage, waiting to be fed
and butchered by their jailer? Who is he, this
captor, that unaided he can keep us in subjection?
They have been calling him a wizard and a

fiend and babbling for days over the mystery of his crime. The devil take his mystery and his wizardy both. He is a man made of flesh and blood and there are three hundred men to face him. We will organize. Let those of able bodies come to the front. And when he appears again, we will fall on him, rush against him, overpower and bind him and be free.

Cries answer. Once more we are on our feet. The general leaps from the rock shelf from which the speakers address us and pushes his way to the front of the cave. We take our places around him and wait. The great rock that fills the entrance will open. He will come again. We stare at the mass of stone remembering how his hands rolled it away as if it were a small and weightless thing. Our leader senses what we are thinking.

"You have heard that it is a trick," he cries. "No human hand can move this rock. Three hundred of us have failed to budge it. It is some engineering trick. Are we children or savages to be cowed by some scientific ruse, some hidden apparatus that works mechanical miracles?"

We wait. Hunger comes again. It is time for our eating. The light that shines mysteriously through the caves is growing dim. Silence has fallen. Suddenly, after our bodies are stiff with waiting, the great rock moves. It turns over and air and twilight fill our eyes. A roar comes from the bull neck of the general.

We stand and tremble. Our leader's hand is raised. It holds a stone in its distended fingers. Those behind us begin to shout. But we in front do not move.

Again we face him. He regards us and we grow weak. He is like a monster that walks on the edge of a dream, calm, waxen, towering. He is dressed in a black robe, girdled at the waist. His feet wear sandals. It is impossible to approach him. I think, as we stand, "is he alive? What power surrounds him? See, we are all trembling before his eyes. A sense of puniness overcomes us."

I recall the fog. It was out of the fog he stole us. Yet it is strange during all the discussions no one has referred to the fog. I alone seem to remember it. This waxen being was in the fog. I can almost remember him, as if I had caught a glimpse of him moving through the annihilated streets. Yes, there is something familiar about this monster. If I have not seen him, I have expected him and for this reason he does not frighten me as he does the others.

I have looked suddenly out of a window, certain that he was standing below, his head raised and waiting for my eyes. I have turned the corner of an empty, sunlighted street, trembling with anticipation, my eyes dreading him. Always I have told myself that were I to encounter him my brain would choke and I would scream; that to encounter his eyes would be to disintegrate, to feel one's soul abruptly erased.

But now as he stands with the stone hills circling beyond him, in the shell of the vanished sun, I feel no terror. The shrewdness with which one becomes an immune slave of monsters who loom out of bad dreams fills my mind. Whatever sort of fiend he is and whatever horrible designs lurk behind his waxen eyes, he will not harm me. He is too powerful and omniscient not to know already that I am his slave, prepared to fawn before him, prepared to yield myself with deliri-

ous and sycophantic gestures to his whims. So why should he harm me?

I smile at him and feel a desire to step to his side and announce myself his ally. But his eyes turn suddenly to me. Cold, malevolent eyes that tear at my brain and surround me with a cloud of horror. Yet in the midst of this shock, even as I feel the impact of his fiendish spirit, a glow of triumph lights my mind. He has not erased me. I close my eyes and sway. I act as the others. But I am only feigning. I pretend that his gaze has devoured me, that I am without thought or volition. And, satisfied, he removes his eyes. Behind the horror left in my senses, is the ecstatic knowledge that I have a weapon against this monstrous one—that I can deceive him.

Furtively I look at those about me. Piltendorff stands with his jaw hanging, his great body limp. The stone has fallen from his hand. Life has gone out of my companions. They are powerless, selfless, inert. Or perhaps they, too, are feigning. It seems to me that the eyes of the poet Julian move slightly. But I will find out about this later.

Suddenly as I stand listening to the forlorn drumming of the sea against the stone hills, a voice sounds. But the voice is not in the air, nor in my ears. His lips have not moved. Waxen, expressionless he stands watching us but he is speaking. I recognize the phenomenon. If he thinks this commonplace miracle will prostrate me he is fooled again. He has transferred his thought to my brain—a telepathic feat I have seen done by ordinary men.

My companions awake. The voice is in them too. A shudder, like a cold wind, passes through the little crowd standing in the valley. Inside our heads is a consciousness of sound. He speaks,

"I am Doctor Sebastien. I am in control of this island and of all who are on it. You are not to disorder your minds with childish thoughts of mutiny. Escape or revolt is impossible. I have brought you here as friends to be co-workers and to share in my kingdom. No harm is to come to you. I will supply your needs. The ten whom I will name are to follow me to my house. Each day ten more are to leave the caves. Those who wait their turn are to have no fear."

The voice ceases. There is no other sound but ten of my companions step forward. The venerable Jacobi is the first. His four colleagues, Meyers, Parks, Potiemkin and Larson follow. And after them move Steinhope, the electrical engineer, Sir Joshua Kane, the physicist, De Morgan, the surgeon, von Rapentov, the psychiatrist, Verelli, the inventor. They are ten of the oldest among us. They approach Doctor Sebastien slowly and with frowning eyes. We hear Jacobi speak.

"We would like to know what the purpose of this outrage is?"

Doctor Sebastien nods and answers.

"Your mission in the Kingdom is to be explained to you."

They walk away toward the stone hills. Darkness obscures their figures. The valley that stretches before our opened cave lies empty and covered with night. We are silent. An exhaustion is in our manner. Slowly we begin to walk toward the entrance of our cave. I linger. Piltendorff, his body rigid, his heavy face scowling and raised to the night, has not moved. I recall how limp and futile he had been under the eyes of Sebastien. But now he is himself again, his bull neck swollen with rage, his fists clenched.

The poet Julian comes to my side. He is a strange creature who has smiled at me whenever our eyes met. He is young and his face is dreamy and beautiful. His presence harasses me and I return his attempt at friendship with precise and uninterested words. Yet he continues to smile at me, as if of all those in the cave I alone was his intimate.

He speaks softly,

"Our Doctor Sebastien fails to impress me," he smiles. "His pose and his display of power just now struck me as rather childish. And I noticed that you too were—"

"You noticed nothing," I interrupt warily, "I am entirely submissive to Doctor Sebastien. He is a powerful and astounding genius."

"Ha," laughs Julian, "you think he will hear what you say of him. That is nonsense. And if he does, what difference does it make? Why not say what you think of him. I do not intend wooing him with long distance flatteries."

"You may do as you please," I answer.

"Why has he brought you and me here?"

Julian continues. "Among this galaxy of obsessed and vicious cranks we are the only two poets."

"I am no poet," I interrupt coldly. He looks at me with gentle and mysterious eyes.

"You are," he says, "and why try to conceal it from me?"

His words startle me. He is someone before whom I must be cautious as I was before Sebastien. His friendliness is menacing.

"Look," he continues, "our general rages in the night. His soul expands with a primitive lust for freedom. The stone hills choke the air he breathes. The others crawl into the caves again, frightened by the night and the memory of this waxen monster it contains. But this man is without fear. He has led great armies. He has chaperoned a million men to their death. He is not like the others in the cave, their brains prowling cautiously over artificial and barely visible tracks. He antedates science. Life has him by the throat and will hurl him against these stone hills, senselessly and remorselessly as it hurled his armies against a plague of cannon and fire. Look. He is about to speak."

In the darkness Piltendorff turns suddenly with his fist upraised and roars at the figures straggling into the cave.

"Comrades," he cries, "are you going back into your holes? He has left the door open. We are free. Halt," he bellows, "come out of there. Follow me!"

Voices answer him indistinctly. He shouts again,

"Fools, cowards, crawling back to your beds. Who is this man that he can hold us like rats in a cavern—with the door open? Come, where is your manhood? We will follow him. We will find his house and tear it down."

The crowd moves. Voices chatter. But none steps forward.

"Would you like to go with him?" Julian whispers.

"No," I answer coldly.

"It would be amusing," his soft voice continues, "We would surprise this fiendish mountebank Sebastien, tie him, truss him up and liberate our friends. It would be pleasing to be free again . . ."

"Stay behind then," Piltendorff cries, "stay

behind and wait like captive children to be fed and butchered. I am going after him. If no one will join me I am going after him alone."

He laughs suddenly at us and shakes his fist toward the cave.

"No man or devil can hold me in his hands like this," he shouts, "goodbye."

Julian has seized my arm.

"Come we will go with him," he whispers.

But I shake him away angrily and he hesitates, his eyes smiling after the general. We watch Piltendorff. He is walking slowly and steadily into the night in the direction taken by Sebastien. His figure grows blurred and disappears in the great shadows cast by the hills. I move back to the cave. He is no longer to be seen. A terror holds me as I think of him moving in the darkness in quest of the monstrous, waxen one who will crush him in his fingers, who will erase him with his eyes. . . There is silence.

"He is gone," Julian speaks, still at my side, "empty handed he walks into the mystery of the island. He will climb the dark hills and bellow his defiance to this man or demon. He will move

[31]

unafraid, shaking his fist at death and terror
. . . I wonder why he was brought here."

The talk in the cave is low. The food
tablets Sebastien has left for us are being distrib-
uted. Our chemists resume their haggling over
the contents of these tablets. Alonzo, the archi-
tect, desires to address us. It has been agreed we
should speak one at a time from the stone shelf.
Alonzo warns us not to eat the tablets. They
contain a drug, he cries, by which the monster
keeps us in subjection. We all witnessed the
working of this drug a few minutes ago . . . But
no one heeds or listens. The food tablets are
swallowed. We are tired of speeches from the
stone shelf. The talk runs on Piltendorff and
on the ten who were taken by Sebastien. What
will happen to them? We have our places to
sleep, and deep in the cave is a swiftly running
river in which to wash.

I desire to be alone and to plan something.
My turn will come soon and I must figure out
how to deceive this monster into treating me
kindly. The persistent Julian has attached himself to me. I am sleepy and his voice drones in
my ears.

"Our turn will come soon," he says, "and this stupid mystery will end. We will both be called together. When the time comes for poets you and I will be called, Mallare. But have you thought of how we came here. We are from all parts of the world. How did he steal us away? Have you thought of this?"

"There was a fog," I answer wearily.

"Yes," he whispers, "white and implacable, like a dream in which the world disappeared. A dream that smelled like an old sea wind. A fog like a great blind moth that settled over the streets and devoured life. Who sent the fog, Mallare? Did it reach everywhere? I was in the street walking and it seemed no more than a mist to me, Mallare. The windows were still blazing. There were vaguely outlined people moving in the fog. It was only a mist. . . A deep breath of rain. . ."

"I want to sleep," I answer this droning poet. "We will talk tomorrow."

"No," he shakes my arm, "let us steal away like Piltendorff. Come, this creature Sebastien will not find us. If he does we can pretend we are asleep and walking in sleep. But it is dark and he will not see us. We will crawl to the top of the hills and be free."

My eyes close. I have no desire to listen to his babbling. He menaces me with his words. Some day I will silence him. I will talk to my huge friend Sebastien about him and repeat his threats and sneers. He grows silent thinking I have fallen asleep. From behind my eyelids I watch him sitting over me, his dreamy, beautiful face smiling at a moon that is shining from somewhere.

[5]

From the Journal of Mallare:—

Day after day passed and we were not called. The cave grew emptier each morning. No word came back of those who were led away and there was no word of Piltendorff. The conviction came to me that something was wrong.

I spoke to Julian. He has been my persistent companion. He remains smiling and amused and talks of Sebastien as if that monster were a ludicrous child.

"When he came that time," I explained to Julian. "I deceived him. I pretended to be obliterated by his eyes. Now I see he knew I was deceiving him. He doesn't trust me. Perhaps he even fears me. That is why I am not called."

Ten by ten our companions left. The cave grew lonely. There were no speeches. Finally the evening of the last ten came. They went, following the strange, yellow-skinned messengers across the valley. I have spoken frequently to Julian of these curious people who arrive with Sebastien's words. They are undersized, effeminate savages. They walk daintily and when they stand still they seem to fall asleep.

"They must be the slaves of Sebastien," I said to Julian on this night when we were left alone. "They are too secretive and unhuman acting to be merely savages. And they look very sad too. They are like weeping girls."

We watched the last of our companions disappear behind their nude and mincing guides. The night rolled slowly over them. As they walked away the valley grew ominous. For the moment I thought I was alone in this stone circled land. A wind was rising. Like an invisible and distracted bird it swooped blindly through the night. I could hear it strike against the hills and return in crazed and disabled leaps. The sea beyond the hills was roaring.

As I stood in front of the cave the valley became filled with wind and noise. Currents of darkness swept past my eyes. Then suddenly a white whip opened the night, thunder drummed out of the sky and the rain came down. Frightened, I stepped into the cave. Julian greeted me. My fingers held his arm.

"Yes," he answered my alarm, "it is going to storm."

His voice was gentle and aloof.

"You are a strange one," I said. "Nothing disturbs you. He has not sent for us. We are alone in this cave now."

"We will wait till the storm grows heavy," he answered, "and then leave this place. It is evident that our captor has no use for us."

I was puzzled. Why had he not sent for us? Here we were alone in this cave, ignored by him. Perhaps Julian was right. When the storm grew heavy we would escape.

The thunder was crackling nearer. Balls of fire pitched through the dark. Vast celestial lanterns swinging through space exploded over the stone hills. Roaring and furious a wall of rain stood in the night. I could no longer hear Julian's voice. He was urging me to follow him into the storm. But the night was falling apart. Our cave rocked with nerve splitting sounds, terrifying miracles of sound to which the ear could no longer listen. I sank down stunned by the detonations. The lightning like insufferable and blazing hallelujahs pierced my senses. Trembling, no longer hearing or seeing I lay torn by the storm. The world seemed to have become a monstrous spark screaming in space.

When I opened my eyes Julian was sitting beside me. The storm still screamed and flared. The wall of rain standing in the night seemed on fire. I stared into this infernal scene and cried out,

"No, we can't go. Look, it burns. We will be blown to pieces."

He lifted me to my feet. We were facing the entrance of the cave and the cloud of horror that is like the shadow cast by Sebastien surrounded me. And suddenly I saw him, drifting in the unnatural night, walking slowly through the terrible crack of thunder—the waxen and towering Sebastien. Julian leaned over me and whispered,

"It is too late now."

He entered the cave. It grew black outside. The rain alone filled the night as if the sea had broken through the stone hills and were running into the valley. Red lights and blue flashes still danced in my head as if my senses no longer believed in darkness. Beside me Julian was talking calmly and with an amusement in his voice.

"It is hardly a night for visiting, Doctor Sebastien. We were just enjoying the little fireworks which preceded your coming. Mallare has fallen asleep. I suggest you do not disturb him. It is late and the rain will fall until morning."

I had sunk to the wet ground. I made no noise now but in the darkness crawled slowly toward the feet of Sebastien. As I neared him the lightning flashed once more and I leaped upright, pointing my hand at Julian and shouting,

"There he is. Seize him before he escapes, Sebastien. He has been tempting me to escape ever since we came here. He does nothing but plot against you. I have no desire to escape. I have been waiting for you patiently and eagerly. It is he who is the plotting one. Seize him. Destroy him before he does us some mischief."

Sebastien said nothing. He turned and we followed him out of the cave into the tumultuous rain. Julian at my side was whispering,

[39]

"It is too late now. He is taking us away."

I scowled and flung his hand from my arm. We stumbled over the water swept grass. I felt peaceful. I smiled in the dark, thinking of the trouble and danger awaiting Julian. For me there would be none. I was Sebastien's friend. He could do nothing that would not please me.

"If he has murdered all my companions," I thought, "It is of no consequence. Their murder was necessary. Perhaps even my murder is necessary. But if he murders me it makes no difference. I am friendly to him. I am one apart from all he has slain."

The house in which Sebastien lived stood beside the sea. We passed through a tunnel in the hills to reach it. It was darkened. I could make out its vast walls, its turrets, its great columns. Inside were groups of the yellow skinned creatures. There were huge elongated windows in the wall. They reached into the darkness of the ceiling. In the corners of the room were pillars around which moved a continual snake-coil of lights. We were given dry robes by the slaves. Innumerable couches made of cushions lined the walls. . .

I felt suddenly tired and at peace. There was an air of peace and well-being in the house of Sebastien. I closed my eyes and fell into a half sleep. He was standing over me but there was no fear in his presence. I was now his slave, a surrendered one stretched before his mercy and he could do nothing while I slept on his couch. Someday I will explore the room and find out the details. The house of which it forms more than half is huge enough to hold thousands of people.

[6]

From the Journal of Mallare:—

We are to build the Kingdom of Evil. It is
for this purpose we were stolen from the world.
All is clear to me now except my own mission
on the island, and the mission of this crazed and
grinning fool, Julian.

The others are at work. They pass in and
out of the great house and beneath the room in
which Julian and I are imprisoned, I hear the
continuous rumble of voices. Lights glare on the
island at night. The stone hills blaze with spectral colors. Explosions waken us at dawn. And
the valley is filled with the strange yellow-
skinned ones running perpetually to and from
the hills.

Since our first talk the night of the storm,
he has concealed himself from us. We will be
called when we are needed, he said. I do not
like the way he associates me with this imperti-
nent and dangerous Julian. How can he think

we are fitted for the same tasks, I who am eager and happy to do his bidding, and this sneering poet who sits and derides him.

At night when the house is silent I talk aloud to Julian, upbraiding him for his disbeliefs and insults. I feel that Sebastien is somewhere outside the window listening. Julian's replies terrify me. It will be thought it is I who say them. Our voices are strangely similar.

"A childish experiment," he laughs, "your friend Sebastien is a charlatan. He bores me with his little airs of mystery. A coquettish fiend he must be, locking us up like this in a room."

As he talks I begin dimly to understand my immediate task. I have been imprisoned with this rebellious and facetious creature in order to change him. With all his power, Sebastien has no influence over Julian. It is I alone who can put an end to his skepticism. I answer him as he sits dreamily regarding me.

"You are a fool, Julian, and unworthy to be present on the island. Here we are to become and to beget a new species of man. ."

"Surgical operations bore me," he smiles. "Come, admit, Mallare, that you are fond of your present contours and that this whole business is a sort of sinister rhetoric with which to frighten children."

I listen patiently and answer,

"You see how you misunderstand the whole thing, Julian. Our clumsy and ineffectual bodies are to be changed but slightly. Let me talk to you about this Garden of Beginnings into which we have been ushered. You do not understand Sebastien or the dream that sleeps behind his waxen eyes."

"Foolish," he murmurs monotonously, "you grow ridiculous, Mallare."

But I continue calmly,

"There will be little change in the body of man. What use is there to change the body? Nature tired of it long ago. She has let man slip from her breast. Now he is no longer an animal suckling in her lap. He is a mind—a phantom stumbling about on incongruous ape legs. And it is Sebastien's plan to release this phantom-man from the terrors and appetites which like an obsolete chrysalis he drags through his days."

"The release of the soul," Julian smiles at me, "is a diversion pleasing to crystal gazers and drug addicts. But you, Mallare, how can you play with such childish and thaumaturgic fancies? . ."

I silence him with a frown.

"In our Kingdom," I speak, glaring into his eyes, "there is to be released not that theological quibble you call the soul but the new monster that has slowly taken form within the shell of man — his mind. You will see what happens then. Miracles and beauties, sins and horrors, will surround us with the thunder of life. A new Genesis will unfold itself within these stone hills."

"Dreams," Julian sighs. "Nonsense invented by ennui. . You play with a poem and lose yourself amid its words."

"Come, Julian," I plead with him, although to what end I cannot tell. For it would be better to cast him loose, or even to kill him. But Sebastien listens outside. It is for this he has locked me in the room with the poet. So I talk.

"See what is happening in the world, Julian. How can you long to escape, to return to that lingering ruin you call humanity? You and I are different. We have been selected to assist at the accouchement in the garden. We have left him behind—man, frightened of this phantom taking birth in him; man, desiring only multiplicity and a sleeping place and clinging desperately to his maggotism. Afraid to tear from himself the chrysalis he has outgrown, he remains, twitching, turning, decaying — a reluctant foetus in the womb of evolution. The new life that writhes within the shell of man will be delivered in this garden, Julian. Mind that hungers for the monstrous companionship of worlds still unknown will spread its wings over these hills. In his world man refuses it birth. Darkly, stubbornly, he clings to his racehood; he hangs on to his humanity when he is already half monster.

"There is a great war going on in the world against mind. Smile at me all you wish. Your eyes cannot make a jest of realities. To this monster that lives in the grey cells of the head, man and his entire baggage of gods, hopes, structures and cunning survival devices, are cumbersome, degenerate impedimenta. And there is this war going on. The monster struggles against its chrysalis. Like a half-born thing, this phantom successor of man struggles to demolish the obsolete and maggoty race that imprisons it. And day and night the world wrestles with this monster whom it fears more than all its wooden gods and iron devils. To what end, Julian? What is the victory man wins over his mind? Madness, my smiling friend. Observe the world we have left. Slowly and inevitably man moves toward madness. The chrysalis is no longer intact. It is ruptured. Decay gleams out of its fibers. Trussed, tied, gagged, flayed and tormented, mind struggles in the panic-stricken grip of man. Denied the logic of birth, denied room for its terrible and exultant wings, this monstrous brother of the gods is beginning to amuse itself with protests. Its clipped and broken wings lift man into crazed circles, tumble him into schizophrenic postures. Its claws scratch at the back of his eyeballs and cause him to see visions, to shriek with fevers, to choke in the embrace of fetid and fellifluous chimeras; to feel insects streaming into the orifices of his body, snakes winding frantically around his genitals, tight bands crunching his bones, fires lighting his intestines. His thoughts denied life, turn into hammers that drive nails into his head, turn into saws whose teeth rip at his arteries, turn into witches that suck his blood, that tear at his organs until screaming with agonies, life ejaculates out of his veins.

"This is man's victory over his mind—madness. Warily, cruelly, he continues his war. You admire him. Yes, how triumphant he seems, this maggoty one. How quiet, how orderly, how noble are his streets and words. Turn your eyes on him, Julian, not on me. Give him your pitying smiles. How smugly man, tortured by laws, shibboleths and philosophies into a brief moment of sanity, postures amid his trophies—a few gods, a few books, a few bottles of medicine. But observe him closely. Behind his pose there is a curious glint. His eyes roll.

"You keep whispering to me to return to this world man has made for himself. You desire I go back and walk in his streets. This is your plot, Julian—the miserable and obnoxious plot that lurks behind your gentle smile. Return me to the world and I become one with the cowled and shivering figures that prowl in dark

[49]

corners. There we are taking form, we spiritual teratisms—a by-product race of man's lies and suppressions.

"You sit here like the effigy of a castaway and your mind is fixed by a single memory. How sweet and pleasant was the companionship of man. This is your dream. You remember him— a sane and charming burgher humming a little tune of well being to himself, scribbling the incessant words humanity and civilization on the sky behind which he has carved his wooden gods. Yes, when I look back I, too, see him and hear his little song. But he is not alone, Julian. Around him gathers a dark, strange company. And Mallare is one of them. A company of cowled and bastard souls—half monster, half man. They circle around him. They close in slowly. And some day they will tear this humming one to pieces. And there will be nothing left in the world but their screams and their black laughter.

"This madness from which I suffer, this will be the end of man. Madness will be his last philosophy. His little song will cease. His monotonous scribblings will end. And mind, the grey and mutilated monster he has enchained within him, will seize his senses. The shapes of life, the noble and complacent structures before which he stands today preening himself and humming will twist into horrible designs, collapse into decalcified symbols of woe. He will weep. Delusions will rupture his nights. Out of the little realities he has so proudly reared, phantoms, ghastly and murderous will launch themselves at him. Everything about him will become laden with horror. The day and night into which he looks will, like dreadful mirrors, give him back only the Witches' Sabbath of his mind.

"Yes, his mind that he crushes today as he thought to crush mine—this grey monster whom he has enchained as a servant for his little vanities and prim altars—this one will leap into his veins, howling and revengeful, and hurl him off his feet. Then the night will see him Julian, and be frightened of him. His world will become a torture chamber through which he will leap, vomiting with terrors. He will look out of bloodied eyes and see only caricatures, ferocious and obscene. The earth will disappear under him and space will become crowded with the torn images of his mind. Wherever he turns he will see only himself. And he will fly, pursued by his despairing and mutilated soul. He will batter himself against hideous walls until hallucinations drag him, snarling and bestial, into a final, terrible mirage.

"Admire him now, Julian. Dream of him wistfully. Plead with me that I return and become one of the shadows cast by his nobility. Reach for my hand to lead me back, unscrupulous friend. But I know the secret of your smile. You would be pleased to see me mad once more. Yes, you are frightened of my sanity in this place. Here on this island where the grey monsters are building their first kingdom you and your little mannerisms become a handful of dust in a high wind. Escape if you desire. It will be best for you. But I am no friend of yours. I belong to Sebastien. The waxen one who never smiles. I have made peace with his terrible eyes. Let him come and take me. Whatever he asks of me I am ready to do. ."

Julian's arguments were silenced. He no longer babbles temptations in my ears as we sleep at night. Apparently he is content to remain in the Kingdom. Now that I have accomplished my first task and silenced this treacherous captive, Sebastien will send for me..

[7]

From the Journal of Mallare:—

There are towers that float high over the stone hills. They hang gracefully in the air like beautifully painted gigantic plumes of smoke. They are made of a substance that resembles colored glass and is more durable than steel or stone.

The first towers to rise in the valley were severe and rectangular. They disappointed me.

"Our Kingdom," I lamented to Julian, "is to be filled with structures that look like warehouse ectoplasms."

But now the new ones are completed. Their shapes are bizarre and pleasing. In the sun they become like a garden hanging out of the clouds. At night they glisten like colossal snow crystals stamped on the darkness and the valley becomes a scene of fairyland shapes.

They are merely a beginning, the workers have explained to me—a few experimental toys for our artists to play with. Indeed, Verelli has perfected a blow pipe which daily surpasses itself in its powers. Julian and I are seemingly the only spectators on the island. We spend our days watching the building operations. He is interested and smiles calmly at the miracles I point out to him.

"Ingenious," he repeats, "the island begins to resemble a permanent firework. Of what use are these structures," he says to the men, "since there is no one to occupy them? To live or to work in such curious buildings would be like inhabiting a Roman candle."

The men do not like Julian. Jacobi frowns when he appears and insists that I keep him away from the chemical sheds in which he and his colleagues supervise the formation of the building substance they call Alphaplasm. But I have persuaded them that Julian will do no harm. It is curious, but I have noticed that the work goes more slowly in his presence. An odd disorganization overtakes the men and they appear to grow confused. The miracles come waveringly from under their hands. For this reason I have resorted to innumerable ruses to escape the companionship of Julian. Some day I shall appeal to Sebastien to put an end to the farce of this crazed and smiling poet's presence in the Kingdom.

There is nothing for me to do as yet but watch the building of these strange streets and towers. Day after day I spend staring at the achievements and inventions of our scientists. An interesting change has come over them. They seem to have lost all memory of their former life. They never refer to their kidnaping, nor to their imprisonment in the caves. I am not allowed to visit their workshops. But from my window in Sebastien's house I can see them. They occupy a vast amphitheater formed by the hills. Within this space there is a continual glare of lights. Terrific clouds of smoke shoot suddenly into the air. Lightnings scream and blaze out of its corners. And behind the fumes and explosions, like children puttering in an inferno, I can see my companions of the caves moving excitedly.

At work on the rearing of towers they chatter to me of discoveries and further plans. But their talk is so vague and involved it seems impossible that they are explaining the wonders unfolding. No coal burns. No hammers or scaffoldings are used in the rearing of the towers. Each one that goes up transcends all its fellows. And a group is already at work demolishing the earlier structures.

The work of demolishing is slower than the building. A long nozzle is turned on the tower. Out of this nozzle leaps a continual fume that reaches in a powerful line hundreds of feet into the air. And inch by inch the structure vanishes under the touch of this mysterious acid.

The building of the towers is accomplished by a dozen men. Verelli's blow pipe of which there are already five on the island, is placed in position. It resembles a great canon. Its energy is generated within an enclosure attached scrotum fashion to its base. Within this enclosure is contained the mystery of the island, the inexhaustible dynamoes with which Sebastien can create or destroy the world at his will.

A massive cistern holds the alphaplasm in its liquid form. Out of the cistern it is forced through a mould and in this mould the substance is given its form. The moulds are fashioned by the artists and are species of architectural microcosm. As the mercurial looking substance pro-

pelled by the blow pipe rises in a slow bubble out of the huge funnel the startling and fantastic designs of the mould are reproduced on a gigantic scale. No sounds are heard during the process. But effortlessly, precisely, as the spider lets out her web, the towers soar out of the funnels. Hundreds of feet in the air they solidify into their snow crystal patterns, complete with stairways, windows, rooms, strange furnitures and capricious and fulgurating ornamentations. Watching these towers grow I feel almost that they are alive, that the substance out of which they take form contains in itself a magical energy. I have talked of this to Julian.

"Our workers," I have argued with him, "are slowly crossing the bridge between organic and inorganic matter. Look at these towers that hover over the valley like a hieroglyph of ghosts. A curious life must breathe within this fluid that rises out of the funnels. Its atoms are alive with geometrical impulses. Fecundated with memories of the mould its cells give birth to fabulous and fluorescent designs. It will not be long before there will be further and more important miracles.

"In these towers they have already created life—a life that blooms fantastically under the urge of the blow pipe; that like some enchanted plant unfolds itself frantically in a single hour of animation. Then, its energies exhausted, it dies. There is something haunting and poignant about their beauty, as if they were mourning the expired dream which gave them birth. Their souls have expended themselves in vast and fragile arpeggios of form. What a puny needlework nature seems beside them. They do not stand but seem to linger like inanimate and crystaline storms in space. In what delirium have such overwhelming castles ever been seen before? Yet watching these geometrical phantoms liberated from matter, you still remain enslaved by the inert and clumsy refuse of the world you have left. See how the valley is taking form, how it becomes daily alive with further enchantments. And it is only just begun. There are mysteries to come which will enrapture and distend our senses. Wait, Julian. You are corrupted by memories. Your smile is a disease that longing has stamped on your lips. But you will change. You will grow like me.."

It is curious that amid all the absorbing developments around me I should remain preoccupied with the reform of this crazed and worthless poet. His obsession of luring me away from the island has inspired him with a dangerous cunning. He mimics my voice and gestures in the hope of bringing down on me the anger of Sebastien and even of the workers, and thus having me expelled from the Kingdom. I have watched him steal away when he fancied I was not looking and seek out Sebastien. Boldly he faces my master and a horror descends on me. He talks to the waxen one with my voice and I lie in a corner shuddering and disappearing as I hear his words.

"You have cast a spell over Mallare," he says. "Release him. Turn your eyes from him for a moment."

And smiling into the terrible eyes of Sebastien he shrugs and turns away. But most of all I do not understand my tolerance of him. I hesitate to demand his death of Sebastien. His dreamy and beautiful face has inspired a repulsive affection in me. Watching him at times as he sits smiling and amused in our room, a deep sorrow overcomes me.

"He is like an exile in this land," I think, "his eyes are dead to its charms. He desires always to escape, to return. He dreams always of another world. He has no soul for this life. How sad he must be under his smile. And what a strange courageous love he has for me."

Thinking this I turn to him and ask,

"Why do you stay, Julian? Why not climb the stone hills and escape alone? You do not belong here. Something terrible will happen to you here. There is still time. You can disappear. Walk away. I am your jailor. But I will turn my back. No one will know. I will conceal it even from him. Why do you not leave, Julian?"

He answers me,

"Because I wait for you, Mallare. Some night we will go together. Without you the world would be empty. I would find nothing in its houses. I would spend the days weeping in memory of you. Here beside you I can smile and wait. There is no hurry, Mallare. The scenes grow pleasant. Enjoy them. But some day we will go back together."

And he looks at me with smiling and longing eyes.

{8}

From the Journal of Mallare:—

I have met Kora. She is the woman whom Sebastien loves. She lives in his house. She is tall, pale and thin lipped. She walks seldom but stands immobile looking out of windows. Her strong and beautiful body is covered with a red robe girdled under her breasts. Her eyes are large and resemble the heads of snakes. Her hair fits like a black mask over her head.

When I come near her she turns and looks at me with contempt and anger. It is almost as if she failed to see me. For many days I was afraid to speak to her. But since the first glimpse of her everything else on the island has lost its lure. I no longer wander about the valley watching the streets and towers come to life. Instead I linger in the great room waiting for Kora to appear. When she has looked a long time out of the windows she will lie down on one of the couches beside the wall. Gradually my courage has increased and I have learned to prepare the cushions for her comfort.

She lies down, ignoring me, her heavy eyes turned upward. I hover at her feet. For days she remained silent. Occasionally her cruel eyes turned to me and her long, thin nose quivered as if she were about to speak. Ah, her eyes! Evil, arrogant and burning, they turn and move in a continual captivity. They stare out of windows. Their lids open and lower as if they were continually retiring into a dream.

"She stands continually before the black doors of her thoughts," I muse as I watch her furtively, and I think of her as she is when Sebastien takes her in his arms. What strange things does he say to her as her body yields itself. What terrible things happen behind the door of the room in which this waxen one takes his bride at night! As I look at her a heavy desire overcomes me. I would like to peer in through the black doors. Her contempt and her anger are the children of a secret.

The yellow skinned slaves bring her fruits and wines. They kneel before her, holding the heavily carved golden platters to her hands.

Stretched on the couch, her chin on her hand, she eats slowly. She drinks wine and her eyes roll upward as if they were unaware of the goblet at her lips. I stand silently at her feet and think, "how wearied and luxurious her gestures are. She is his bride. How horrible his kisses must be. His lifeless mouth feeding on her lips. Yet she is not afraid of him. She turns memories over and over in her mind. Behind the black doors are capricious and demonaic figures. Her eyes stir sleepily like the heads of snakes lifting out of a pantomime of lusts."

At times Julian appears. He walks smiling into the room, his expression lighting as he sees me standing motionless at her feet. But each time I gesture him away with a frown. He ignores her. But when he appears Kora awakes from her lethargy. Her eyes glow and turn in her head. Her thin lips stretch into a brooding grimace and her nostrils quiver. She lifts her symmetrical and elastic hand and allows her fingers like little snakes to trail lasciviously over her hidden breasts. Julian's eyes avoid her. He remains looking at me, pleading and amused.

[69]

One day she spoke to me. Julian had come into the room. She was looking at him as her voice, harshened with satiety, addressed me.

"What is your name?"

"Mallare," I answered.

"You are the new slave?"

"Yes," I said.

"Who is that man who comes in here and smiles at you?"

"He is the poet, Julian."

I had left my place at the foot of her couch and was standing in front of her.

"Kneel when you speak to me," she murmured.

I knelt and raised my face to her. For a long time she stared at me, her eyes heavy and miserable with weariness. I could feel her mind crawling with angers. A lascivious fear excited me. Suddenly she raised her hand and struck my face.

"The sight of you disturbs me," she frowned. "Your eyes are too sick and fawning. Wherever I turn there are eyes like yours. Crafty and malignant eyes fill this Kingdom. Who has given you permission to stand by my couch?"

"No one," I whispered.

"You are a repulsive slave," she muttered. "Your face is deathly pale and your eyes gleam with a continual fear. At first I thought you were a man. But I see you are like the rest of these fawning and infatuated invalids that serve me. You, too, are thin and furtive. You wander about like a ghost."

She paused and a laugh muttered on her lips.

"I am tired of ghosts," she went on broodingly. "Images that burn in a continual sleep. Look, he surrounds me with hallucinations. His mind hatches them—whining, trembling fools like you; phantoms with frightened and melancholy gestures. For whom does he build this Kingdom? All these towers are mine. Later he will fill the valley with monsters with which I may disport myself. But why do I talk to you?"

Her eyes were resting heavily on Julian. Her body moved under its red robe as if in pain.

"You are not a man," she whispered harshly, "but that one over there is different. He resembles you. Yes, his face and his body are like yours. But he is different. His eyes are not sick.

[73]

He belongs to another world. He smiles tolerantly at us. Where did he come from?"

"I do not know," I answered.

"What can he want in this valley?" she continued. "Ah, I desire him."

She lowered her eyes to me and frowned.

"Do you understand?" she murmured. "I desire him. He is different from all the rest. But he refuses to look at me. Unfasten the girdle of my robe, Mallare. Lift it from my body. I want him to see me. He will look at me then."

I obeyed with bewildered hands.

"Do not look at me," she commanded harshly. "It is for Julian I uncover myself."

I knelt with closed eyes before her naked body.

"Ha," she sighed, "how proud he is. There is blood in his veins. He refuses to turn this way. Run after him, Mallare, tell him I desire him. I want to feel his heavy, flesh covered hands on me. Ah, you fool, he is gone."

Her palm struck violently against my face.

"Wake up," she cried excitedly. "Look at me now. Study me carefully so that you may

describe all my charms to him. What am I like,
Mallare?"

"You are like a white candle burning in a
horrible room," I answered.

"Yes," she murmured.

"You are an evil woman sleeping amid
dreams," I wailed, "your body is a ghostly
couch. Your breasts are the white jewels of
passion."

"Tell him these things," she whispered.
"He will listen to you even if he refuses to look
at me."

Her hand seized me by the hair and raised
my head.

"Do you understand?" she cried. "I desire
him. If you do not persuade him to come to me
I will have you killed."

"You are cruel," I answered, unable to look
at her any longer. "Let me kiss your hands and
you may kill me. Let me stay where I can look
at you and I will kneel before you till I die of
desire."

"You will tell him how white and inexhaustible my flesh is," she repeated harshly, "and
how at the sight of me you were overcome with

desire, ready to spend your life for a caress from my hands. But tell him no man has ever yet touched me. Only fevers and dreams have breathed their lusts over me. None but sickly and prowling ones like you have come to my feet. Yes, even Sebastien. I am sick of shadows, I would betray him for a man."

I reached my arms to embrace her. Her eyes halted me. In their rage I grew weak and frightened.

"You dare to touch me," she spoke slowly.

The heavy girdle flashed from her side. It fell across my back. I closed my eyes. Blows were cutting my flesh. She had risen from the couch and was standing over me. Something hideous and unreal came into the scene.

Pain and terror transfixed me at her feet. Unable to cry out or move, I opened my eyes and for a moment it seemed that not Kora but the malevolent figure of Sebastien was towering over me. The air gleamed with the jewels of her swinging girdle. But I could no longer see her. I struggled to call her name, to send my voice out of the paralysis in which I lay. Sharp hands were reaching into my body. They lifted me up, pulling me through the air. I became like something crushed and dismembered in a dreadful flight. Then suddenly I began to sink, to drift happily to the ground. For moments I lingered ecstatically at the end of this strange ride.

When I rose from the floor she was clothed in her robe, its girdle stained with my blood. She lay heavy lidded on the couch. For moments she regarded me sleepily.

"Go now," she said at length. "You have found out how beautiful I am. Tell him what I have done to you. Yes, when he sleeps crawl close to him and whisper in his ear that as I flayed you, my veins were hungry for his strange and solid flesh. Go bring him to me."

Two of the yellow slaves appeared.

"Take him away," she commanded.

They supported me through the room. As I moved forward I saw Sebastien. He was standing behind one of the pillars. Kora, undulant, her shoulders raised, her hands caressing her body, was gliding toward him. A tender, fawning light was in his eyes.

"Whose blood is on your girdle?" he murmured.

"Mallare's," she laughed.

She seemed to crouch before him, her hands moving sinisterly on the air, their fingers spread and bent back.

"And where is he going?"

"I have sent him on an errand," she whispered. "He is a pleasing slave. I prefer him to these yellow and bodyless creatures."

I moved on, afraid to look back. She desired Julian. She preferred him to me. His overbearing manner had excited her. She was ready to betray Sebastien for him. I almost wept with these thoughts.

Julian was waiting for me. He greeted me with a brooding smile.

"What do you want to say to me?" he asked softly as I remained silent.

"Nothing," I answered.

"No. You keep looking at me. She has instructed you to tell me something and you are afraid."

"Nothing more than that she despises you," I muttered, "and that she does not want you prowling around the room in which she lies.

She is mine," I raised my voice. "It is I who found her, not you. It is my eyes that saw her, not yours. Keep away from her."

"So you have succumbed to this whip flourishing andromaniac," he smiled. "You, Mallare, who have been too proud to lower your lips to virgins. And this is one of the delights of the Kingdom you keep promising me—a sulphurous strumpet whose eyes puff and narrow like expiring toads; an obscene husk of flesh stewing in a caldron of desire. You are content to join the yellow skinned hermaphrodites that fawn about her, to let her foul your body with the blows of her girdle. So this is your mission in this fine Kingdom—to be a slave whimpering at the feet of a sexual paroxysm."

I struggled against the words forming themselves in my mind. But it became imperative to speak them. It was as if her eyes were again menacing me, as if her hands again threatened the dreadful flight.

"Yes, at her feet, Julian," I cried. "It is not I she desires but you. I must bring you to her."

We looked at each other and in this moment I knew that I would some time kill him. His smile was gone and there was only hate in his eyes. I grew frightened of him and moved away as he came closer to me murmuring.

"What a fraud you are, Mallare. Babbling of your dreams; flying from life to posture amid the shadows of your mind. And I like a fool following you. For I, too, was tired of life. It was you, Mallare, who seduced me with the whisper of gates beyond which lay a Kingdom of evil miracles. If I would be silent you would create a world for me. I let the fog devour us, Mallare. I let this ringmaster Sebastien steal your senses. Ha, and what has happened? Spermatazoic towers and venereal rainbows spawn like a foul vegetation out of your madness. And this you call the superior and beautiful dream man denies himself—this montonous architecture of lusts, this phallic circus through which you prance like a castrated satyr. And now Kora, the inevitable strumpet, appears. Ah, Mallare, I am bored with your madness. Your erotic decorations begin to weary me. The valley into which you have tumbled is a yonic pit. The mind you have released creates no more than a burlesque bed for harlotries."

As he talked he came close to me and now with his face almost touching mine I realized he was mad and that I must smile at him and be cautious while he raged.

"There is no Mallare," he whispered. "I am Mallare. I whom you call Julian and who follows you like a shadow, I am all that lives. Everything else in this Kingdom, including you, is a phantasmagoria I tolerate and at which I have smiled too long. It is in my power to blot out this lewd mist. All the horrors and monstrosities at which you are beginning to tremble, I have only to wave my hand and command them and they will crawl back into my mind again, dragging you after them."

We stood facing each other for a long time in silence. Then he shrugged and, the smile returning to his lips, walked away. I understand this crazed and babbling poet now. He fancies he is a superior version of me. He is like a wraith speaking out of a mirror demanding that I disappear in order that he may steal my identity. He is jealous of me. In this Kingdom he is nobody. His clumsy senses are unable to embrace the mysteries that surround him. Angered by the impotency he feels he is beginning to boast of his powers. The convenient fancy has come to him that he is the source of life, the chrysalis of Mallare. He goes around smiling idiotically to himself and now he begins to threaten me with his delusions.

But I will have to be careful. He is not as great a fool as he makes himself out. He has a certain cunning. He mimics me well. At times he even steals my words and talks in such a manner that I stare at him confused by his similarity. It becomes obvious that he will have to be destroyed or some day he will overpower me when my back is turned. He will dress himself in my clothes and escape. He is growing involved and capricious and I will have to be on my guard lest his madness causes something dangerous to happen.

Yet why does she desire this crude and heavy fool? What is there in him that is not in me? She dreams of him continually. She thinks his boasts are real. She does not see he is an impostor. Or perhaps she desires merely to torture me.

I begrudge her no pleasures. Yet I cannot endure her love for Julian. I do not mind what
sins she commits. She will some day prowl
through the towers. There will be fresh couches
and new slaves for her in every room. Hour
after hour, day upon day without pause, she will
feed hungrily on bodies—a single woman avora-
cious and inexhaustible, among a kingdom of
men. But all this I do not mind. I begrudge her
nothing. I will follow her, waiting humbly for
her embrace. Only Julian is my rival. His arms
alone can take her from me. If he goes to her
couch I will die of anguish.

The days passed. Julian no longer followed
me. We talked little. He would question me at
times of the things happening in the valley, and
when I answered vaguely he would smile, under-
standing that I had been with Kora. But he refused to mention her.

"He is becoming reconciled," I thought.
More and more I began to ignore him. But one
night I woke from a deep sleep to find his hands
reaching for my throat. He was leaning over me
and muttering,

"With my fingers I can bring all these chimeras tumbling out of their black sky. I can put an end to this maniacle farce."

I lay feigning sleep and waited. His hands dropped. His eyes, filling with tears, he swayed his head back and forth and murmured,

"She will take him from me. Oh, Mallare, how far will your infidelities lead you?"

I was about to spring up and answer him when I saw Sebastien. His waxen face was looking in through the tall window. Never have I seen him more horrible. But his eyes were not on me. They stared at Julian. Malignant and ferocious, they blazed behind the tall window waiting for Julian. Unable to breathe, I watched the poet turn his face slowly.

"Yes," he whispered, "I see you, Sebastien —the fiend that walks the edges of Mallare's dream. You have come for me, eh? You do not like the threats I have been making. You are afraid I have followed him into the dark land he calls your Kingdom for no good purpose. You are beginning to wonder why I, who do not belong here, linger like a powerless and mournful companion beside his night."

[84]

He paused and the two regarded each other. Julian spoke again.

"Yes, I must sit by, smiling miserably at your mountebank tricks, Sebastien. Amusing myself amid the weird hoaxes by which you seduce and enslave him. How horrible you seem to him. Even in his sleep now he trembles."

As he whispered Julian approached the tall window. He was changing. His voice no longer purred. His smile was gone. The face of Sebastien had pressed itself against the glass.

"Come inside," Julian cried suddenly. "You, Sebastien! Come inside. And bring them all in —the entire army of chimeras that flow from your waxen eyes. I will destroy them one by one to the last of your abominations. I will tear down each tower you breathe into the air. Come, my glowering monster, bring ·in your lecherous bride and your androgynous slaves to defend you. I am going to tear your little Kingdom down."

Then a queer thing happened. Julian was yelling in front of the tall window and beating on it with his fists. Yet the glass did not break.

He hurled himself at the walls, banging with his feet and with his arms swinging over his head. Like a blind and powerful beast he rushed from door to window. But nothing moved under his attack. The face of Sebastien remained looking at him behind the unbroken glass. I closed my eyes and tried to withdraw from the scene. But the figure of Julian continued clear. Blood was beginning to cover him. He seemed like a madman raging in a cell of shadows. The walls and windows against which he battered ignored him and gave out no sound as if he did not exist for them. Yet in his frenzy Julian kept screaming,

"Come inside, Sebastien. Bring them inside. I will tear them to pieces. Wake up, Mallare. Look, I am destroying them all. You are free."

Still shouting these words he sank to the floor, his hands clawing at the air. I watched him till he grew still. He lay at the foot of the tall window behind which Sebastien had watched his impotent assault. His robe was torn and as I approached him furtively I noticed that the flesh of his back was cut into long bruises. I stood over him and smiled. How ridiculous his

[86]

attack had been. There was little to fear after all from this treacherous poet. Whatever his powers were, they were of no avail against the flimsiest barriers of the Kingdom. His gestures were empty as sentences that have no meaning.

"What a humorous megelomaniac this worthless creature becomes," I thought. "Boasting that he will destroy our Kingdom. Ha! His rage and cries have not even disordered the curtains of the room. His wildest blows made less an impression on these walls than the feet of an insect crawling over them."

He stirred as I stood watching him. Opening his eyes for a moment he saw me and muttered,

"I have destroyed them, Mallare. You are free. They are gone."

I said nothing. The door against which he had battered in vain opened easily to my hand. I left him lying brokenly where he had fallen. The night like a black ghost moved among the pillars outside the room. There were no sounds. A desire I could not resist carried me along, lifting my feet down the flight of stairs. In the darkness at the foot of the stairs I paused.

The vast room was illumined with heavy colors. Lights twinkled in its corners. I waited, confused by the acrid odors that suddenly filled the place. Humid and cavernous, the chamber seemed to be drawing me into it. I could no longer walk on its floor. My feet slid under me and I floundered amid cushions that crawled with life under my hands.

"This is a dream," I thought, "something queer has happened. This room has never been like this before. It is alive. It yields under my touch. Its walls breathe."

I would have turned and gone back to the dark stairs. But fetid and pulsing shadows enclosed me. I shut my eyes and continued to move forward. Then out of the dark I heard a voice.

"Mallare.."

She was lying against one of the windows, her body raised high by cushions.

"Why do you stop," she called again, "are you afraid?"

I stared and trembled. A dim light glittered about her. Her hair made a wavering arc around her head, floating on the air like the coiffure of a drowned woman.

"Have you brought him?" she whispered. "I have been waiting.."

Then suddenly her arm, white and straight, lifted itself out of the dark. In her hand was a serpent. Its whip-like body uncoiled itself slowly and stretched a flattened head toward me.

[9]

From the Journal of Mallare:—

We have been busy with our God. It was Kora who desired him first. This happened one day when we were being carried through the valley in her litter. She is never tired of riding on the shoulders of the hermaphrodites. Resting on her elbow amid the inevitable cushions, she lay regarding me as I squatted at her feet, holding the litter curtains apart that she might see the streets.

"You find these scenes beautiful, Mallare?" she muttered.

Her eyes for the moment had lost their cruelty. Her proud lips wavered into sadness. I answered,

"Yes. I never grow tired of watching the streets. It seems to me that the towers grow daily higher, more involved and opalescent."

"They are empty," she gestured me to drop the curtain. "What a fool you are, Mallare.

These little toys suffice you. You dream of nothing else."

"Of you," I whispered.

"I am weary of being dreamed of," she answered heavily. "Of what use are these towers. They, too, dream of me. Empty miracles that have no meaning."

"None but beauty," I said.

"There is no beauty," Kora answered. "When the nerves tire of accidents the thing you call beauty vanishes."

"You never vanish, Kora."

She ignored me, saying,

"One desires always something more mysterious than oneself. To you I am a dream. Behind my eyes is a world alive with terrible and unimagined figures. You come crawling to the black doors of my mind. When I grow angry and strike you, the doors, unguarded, open for the instant and from under the torture of my blows you peer in and see...what do you see, Mallare?"

"Nothing."

"What do you see?"

Her eyes were commanding. Unable to endure them I hid my head in the cushions and waited for her rage. Instead there was silence. She sighed and continued,

"Ah, to behold something I dare not name! Of what use are the miracles Sebastien performs for me? They provide only new and more complicated sources of ennui. His slaves who kneel and posture around me, his aphrodisiacle towers and glittering streets. Yes, he embraces me with ingenious and diabolical gestures. And he has brought you to my couch. For moments these things distract me from my emptiness. In the illusions and terrors I inspire in others I find a brief pleasure. But even this adds to my despair. You have wondered at my cruelty, Mallare. Let me tell you the secret of my anger. A strange rage overcomes me when I see your fawning, worshipful eyes raised to me. I grow angered because your eyes see something hidden from mine. I am jealous of the illusions I inspire in your head. To you I am a world unknown, a hypnotic altar before which you abase yourself. When I see you thus a fury possesses me. I would slay you because you worship me. I am jealous, I tell you, of the dream I inspire in you. It is a

[95]

rival before whom I feel small and empty. This is why I beat you. When you lie fainting under my blows it is not you I have slain for the moment but the beauty and mystery you miscall by my name. Each sigh you raise to me, each desire that bends you to my feet is an infidelity I must punish. Ah, to you I am a Goddess, mystic, unattainable. To myself I am an overfamiliar and monotonous shadow."

She paused and I answered,

"I know well who you are, Kora. If I worship you it is not as you think. I am a slave in your eyes yet I am very clever. More clever than anyone else on this island. Yes, as clever as Sebastien. I know who you are."

"Who am I?" she asked softly.

"You are the delirium out of which life is born," I answered her, "the sob of pleasure which ejects all living things into the world. You ask what I have seen behind the black doors. You are right. They have opened and I have beheld your soul, Kora, the poisonous kiss of ecstasy which translates pleasure into matter, which for a brief moment casts a ridiculous enchantment over the chemistries of flesh. Julian, the poet whom you still desire, talks of you in crude and embittered words. His clumsy senses behold in you merely an eternal harlot."

"What else does Julian say, Mallare?"

"He is mad, quite mad. His mind struggles sadly within the shell that chokes it. At night I listen to him babbling that you are the mirage that rises out of the sewers of life when they have run dry. He speaks of you in ugly phrases."

"It is true. He is right. I am a shadow, Mallare."

"Ah, weary of wounding me, Kora, you turn now upon yourself in quest of deeper satiety. See how real you are," I smiled, taking her hands, "have I not felt your blows?"

She stared at me heavily.

"Yes, if you are sad, Kora," I continued, "it is because your soul longs for exhaustion. You become like an orgie whose last and hopeless hunger is for sleep."

"This Kingdom is empty," she murmured. "I can no longer endure it. I will persuade Julian to lead me away."

"You desire to return to the world," I frowned, "what marvelous thing will you find growing out of that dung heap that is not in this valley?"

"God," she answered. "One to whom I can turn, as all others turn here to me. You are right, Mallare. My soul gasps in an endless Saturnalia. Behind the black doors a useless orgy continues. Sebastien has stolen me for his bride. Together we lie in inexhaustible embraces. He invites his slaves into my soul. Things of which you may never dream transpire. And like you, too, he whispers to me that I am the final one, that he builds his Kingdom for me, that beyond me there is nothing and less than nothing. When he leaves me I wander about looking out of windows. Neither you nor even Sebastien are my lovers. There is One else. Your friend Julian reminds me of Him. I remember someone else— a thing to which I turned; a God whose presence transformed the monotonous frenzy of my soul into a secretive, meaningful ritual. I desire a God over this Kingdom, Mallare. Without a God I cannot endure my corruption nor hide trom it. I will tell this to Sebastien tonight. If a God does not come to his Kingdom I will leave it."

[10]

From the Journal of Mallare:—

Thus it was we began work on the God. A silence fell on the amphitheater in the hills. No more smoke or flame rose out of the stone bowl. Tirelessly the hermaphrodites ran to and fro in the valley. Again I was bidden to remain in my room and again the great hall below was crowded with the workers come to confer with Sebastien. I sat with Julian listening to their voices rumbling. I sought vainly to reach Kora to find out what was happening. Twice Sebastien came to my window and I besought him for explanations. But, as before, he paid no heed to me and stood regarding Julian from behind the glass.

Then one day the Temple began to rise. Julian and I watched it appear. It was not like the other towers. It began coming out of the earth like a colossal plant. It made a green circle a mile in circumference. Julian smiled as we watched it growing from day to day.

"At least," he said, "it is different from the architectural spasms they have been blowing into the air. Your gingerbread castles were beginning to give my eyes an indigestion. I can no longer look at them without feeling optically ill."

It was not until weeks had passed, however, that we were able to understand the significance of the new structure. Then as the green walls climbed precipitously into space, the Temple acquired a cylindrical terror. It became daily more impossible to look at its curved and looming walls. Higher and higher they mounted until their monotony blinded the eye. There were no windows, nor apertures; no decorations nor interruptions. One gazed futilely at its monstrous lines and grew dizzy as if one's eyes were sliding frantically into space.

Then when it had ascended to an incalculable height, its summit began to bloom. We could not at first distinguish what was happening. But gradually tremendous and undulating shapes began to spread over our heads. A flower

that was like a sky was taking bloom out of this
terrible spire. It unfolded itself in gigantic petals that blazed with colors. It extended itself
into trumpeting designs, into a whirl and explo-
sion of patterns that brought us to our knees as
if a hurricane had burst over us.

It was no longer possible to walk near the
Temple. Even Julian shut his eyes to it. The
workmen crept on their hands and knees around
it and lay for hours flattened against the earth.
A perfume began to fill the Kingdom. In the
morning a rain of odors descended on the valley
and through the day and night a strange sound
that was like the rumble of distant seas came
from within the terrifying walls.

When it stood completed Sebastien alone
was able to approach its shadows. He walked
slowly toward a door invisible to us. He seemed
to shrink as he drew closer to it and several times
we saw his knees bend as if the colossal sym-
metries were hammering him to the earth. He
entered at last. We waited for him to emerge
and when night came he was still inside. I began to grow frightened. Sitting with Julian in
our room I stared at the structure that remained

forever inconceivable to my eyes. In the darkness it looked like a world.

"Perhaps it has devoured Sebastien," I murmured. "He has not come out yet."

Julian pointed. I looked out of the window again. An object that seemed microscopic was moving away from the black walls. It was Sebastien crawling on his hands and knees. We watched him stagger to his feet and walk slowly toward our house.

"It is a flower," Julian mused, regarding me with eyes which have grown troubled of late. "A gigantic and perfect flower."

"Yes," I assured him, "it is nothing more. Our scientists whom you deride so childishly created a seed out of which it grew. There were days when watching it mount from the earth, they were filled with terror, not knowing how high it would climb or whether the island would be able to support it. But now you see it finished and in bloom. It is hollow inside, I am told, although no one has been able to enter it and see—except Sebastien. It will require a long time for us to become innured to its overwhelming proportions. It will be months, perhaps

years, before we can raise our eyes to enjoy the
great flower that swoops from its summit."

It was with Kora that I first entered the
Temple. I had been standing beside her couch
in the now familiar room where she spends the
day. Her eyes had of late been glittering with
excitement.

"Come," she said suddenly, "I can wait no
longer. I am impatient to see what is inside. We
will have to walk. The slaves are not yet able
to approach its door."

Holding my hand, she pulled me along
toward its walls. As we came near to them a
paralysis crept into my body. There was no
sound or movement yet flame and thunder
seemed falling from the terrible walls.

"I cannot," I whispered, "tomorrow.."

Kora's arm circled me. She was trembling.

"No," she commanded, "walk."

Fainting under the rush of wall over my
head, I stumbled beside her through a door. For
an instant my eyes remained open to the scene
that assailed them. Then quickly a blindness
came, as if they had been torn out of my head.

When I recovered Kora was lying against me, her arms burying me in her breasts.

"Do not look," she spoke in my ear, "not yet. Wait till you are prepared."

I lay quivering and chilled despite her embrace. I could hear the walls of the Temple roaring around us.

"They are alive and white," she continued. "I cannot raise my eyes to them yet. Listen.. life is screaming through them."

Slowly my ears began to choke with tumult. A pendulum of sound swooped and crashed from wall to wall. As I lay gasping I realized there was neither heat nor light nor even noise about me; that my senses were struggling with strange impacts. Space, imprisoned within the walls, leaped toward an invisible roof and tobogganed down the towering sides—a space fecundated, bellowing and sledge-like, pounding with invisible hammers at the circle of walls. The Temple was quivering as if its tremendous stalk were about to burst.

"Come, stand up," cried Kora. "We are in the midst of life."

I rose and crouched, unable to straighten my body beside her.

"Who but a God could live in here?" she continued exultantly. "Even I would expire within these walls. And Sebastien, who lingered here a few hours, lay almost dead when he returned. Look, Mallare, behold it. It is like a colossal vein, beating with cataracts and disappearing into space."

I no longer heard her words. She was pulling me over the moving ground.

"We must get out of here," I shouted, "or we shall be torn apart."

It was night when we emerged. Beyond the shadow of the Temple we fell exhausted and lay for a long time. Finally Kora prodded me to my feet. We walked slowly to Sebastien's house. Kora was silent. I shivered as I looked at her eyes.

"You are thinking of the God that is to inhabit the Temple," I murmured.

She answered nothing. I left her on the couch surrounded by kneeling slaves who raised heavily carved golden platters. Her eyes closed over the wines and fruits offered. She lay smiling and caressing herself as I moved away.

"I have been in the Temple," I whispered to Julian.

"Yes? What is it like?" he asked.

"It is white and alive, like the inside of a flower," I answered. "One cannot stand up. We were there for hours but I saw nothing. My eyes refused to look at the walls. All is silent inside and a thick light glares evenly. Yet an inferno sucks at your senses."

I paused as he smiled, shaking his head.

"Ah, my sneering one," I cried, "what derisions have you for this building? It is His Temple, the dwelling place of a God whom we do not yet know. Does this, too, amuse you as did the streets and towers?"

"Yes," he answered.

I regarded him pityingly.

"Then wait," I replied, "wait for the One who is to sit on this white throne."

"For a God," he continued to smile. "Mallare asks me to prepare my knees for a God. Have you forgotten, Mallare? I have always laughed at Gods whether they inhabit caverns, skies or even flowers. Gods are the last fantastic outlines man gives to his delusions. Aztec Gods, Gods that danced to Babylonian cymbals, jungle Gods that walk with typhoon feet, pale Gods that whimper on Crosses, dragon headed Gods that spawn in Asian caverns, Gods of Egypt, Athens and Rome—ah, Mallare, what Gods have there not been? Man has worshipped his every terror and every dream in Temples as strange and horrible as this one. When his hands were still too clumsy for caresses, when his mind was still too new to name the things it encountered, he was already old and adept in the building of altars. He built them of ice amid glaciers, of stone, iron, gold and forgotten metals amid hills that have disappeared. In the midst of life he has raised always the macabre stages on which the melodrama of dream and terror has played itself.

"And now you come with another God, Mallare. The grey monster you have released is not enough. The mind of whose infinities you babble needs explanations beyond itself. Ah, Mallare, if you must entertain your illusions with Gods let them at least be humorous like the totems of savages. Let them be toys for a mantel-piece. Let them be ironical and amusing Gods such as we can destroy; little Gods who will ask questions of us; Gods like pretty dolls to decorate our philosophies."

"Enough," I silenced him. "You talk like a fool. There have been no Gods yet. Temples, perhaps, have waited for them. But none has come. Have you ever seen a God, Julian, you who prattle of an encyclopedia of Gods? Yes, you smile. I know your answer. The minor poets have always one answer. They have heard the murmur of a God in winds and seen His eyes in stars and felt His hands reaching in caresses out of dawns. You have never seen a God and you make little poems out of your disillusion. Yes, man has haunted himself with the fear and love of Gods. His mind has tormented him with mysterious cries and grotesque shapes to which he has given the name of Gods. But when, Julian, has he dared to face the God toward which his nature drags him, reluctant and terrified, through time?

"Wait," I cried, glowering at him, "it is Kora, not I, who has asked for One to worship.

Kora, who is sickened with dreams and who desires to see a God, to kneel before Him as he sits on a throne in the Temple. And this Temple whose walls roar above our island is not a stage for shadows but a terrible home into which a God is to come. Mad though you are, you will not smile when you see Him."

{11}

From the Journal of Mallare:—

Julian will no longer walk on the island. There are things happening that offend him. He was amused at first by the garden that has appeared around the Temple. But now he refuses to enter it. I too hesitate to return but it will be necessary soon to join the holiday that is being prepared in the garden.

Flowers as tall as high trees bloom in a grove that circles the Temple. When one walks through the grove the blossoms drift overhead like great colored balloons. Beneath this vast roof of petals that shuts out the sun the grove stretches in a maze of bending pillars. Thousands upon thousands of stems rise in identical and towering pipes of green, in elongated arcs that cross and interloop until the grove spins with spherical spaces and seems like a collision of whirling tops. One grows dizzy moving among the snarl of curves. The great stems bewilder one like a confusion of parentheses and in the distance the grove becomes a scribble of lines that entangles the eye. The air, without sun, is green and dim and steams with odors almost too heavy to breathe.

Here we walked during the first days. Our eyes tormented by the multitude of attenuated arcs refused after an hour to lead us further. As if whirled off our feet we would sink to the earth and lying thus, watch the grove circle over our heads into its high roof of flowers.

"I would admire your botanists more," Julian complained, "if they did not vie with merry-go-rounds and ferris-wheels. How the devil can one enjoy a garden that teeters and spirals in front of one's eyes?"

Nevertheless he returned, lured like myself by the elliptical forest of stems. It was after many visits that we came upon the first of the monsters. It was a strange looking acephalic thing no larger than a child. It crawled and rolled toward the Temple wall. Julian watched it and said nothing. Through the monotonous roar that fills the grove near the Temple came suddenly the cries of the hermaphrodites. We turned and saw numbers of them hunting among the bending flower trunks.

"It is something that has escaped," I whispered to Julian. "Look, it is going to climb."

We watched the headless thing as it began crawling like a white slug up one of the flowers.

When we returned a few days later to walk again in the grove Julian was oppressed and nervous.

"I do not like the sounds in here," he muttered, "and it seems to me I see things in the distance. I no longer trust you, Mallare."

He followed me reluctantly. After a half hour he seized my arm and cried out.

"The place is alive with hideous shapes. Look, over there. And all around us."

A ball of flesh that resembled a huge and dismembered octopus lay in our path. Its sides ballooned and collapsed as it breathed. Suddenly it moved, rolling over, and we saw a great mouth surrounded by growths and perforations. Red, membraneous lips hanging like barrels opened and a tongue emerged and beat like a gong between them.

Julian turned away quickly. But he remained without moving. Around us in every direction were dreadful, nauseating figures; two-headed things with faces drooping at the ends of wilted stalks; creatures with boneless limbs and bodies like pouches; creatures with swollen and pendulous heads riveting them to the earth; animate snail-like masses of flesh, hair-matted and mucous-covered; thick, serpent-like bodies that struggled to stand erect; half-formed heads that raised themselves above appalling disfigurements. I could not believe them alive at first and thought they must be matter that had erupted fungus fashion out of the earth. But staring I detected amid these obscene and tumorous shapes, horrifying human fragments —the arm of a man, the perfect breasts of a woman; human eyes staring out of putrescent and formless growths, human lips red and grimacing in swollen smiles. Around us they crept, emitting sounds, clawing at the air with fingers and stumps—a convulsive debris of faces, limbs and fetal distortions moving like foul bags of life.

Julian fled. I stood unable to move until one of them, tall as a man, its bulbous head rising out of a discolored sack of flesh, turned its face toward me. For the moment I looked at it a horror contracted my skin. I saw stamped upon this hideous growth and half-hidden by a cowl of skin a face I knew—a face with melancholy eyes and wide brooding mouth; a man's face, perfect and thinking, its hair falling in a black slant across its brow.

"My face!" I screamed.

I leaped away as it crept toward me. It moved as if legs were buried within it. I heard Kora calling my name and opening my eyes saw her standing before me.

"So you are afraid," she spoke harshly, her hand gripping me.

"There was one who looked like me," I answered. "I saw his eyes. He turned to me."

"You were dreaming," she interrupted. We walked together. Noises followed us.

"Where have you been?" I murmured. "I have haunted the grove looking for you."

"I have been with the workers in the hills," she answered, "watching these strange figures

spawn out of tubes and retorts. They are tiny
when they come out and resemble mutilated
dolls. But they grow quickly. In a few hours
they swell to the size of children and men. Over-
night they become massive. There are some you
have not seen—the old ones. They lie like great
stranded hulks protruding from the sea. The
water has not yet drowned them. They breathe
and at night they emit sounds."

I was silent. Her voice grew exultant.

"I have asked for a God and they are creat-
ing one," she continued. "They have discovered
how to put life together. And for weeks, day and
night, I have watched these monsters bloom, each
like a fecundated piece of flesh that struggles to
take the shape of a man and collapses into a
miserable caricature. At first there were only
things that resembled tumors. They swelled into
great bubbles of meat out of which bones and
organs protruded. These were cut open and inside, ah Mallare, inside there was life. There
were cells bathed in faint trickles of blood.
There were things that looked like hands and
even faces and veins throbbing around long
pieces of bone. The workers cut them open with

gleaming eyes. They cut and scraped and poured new drops of fluid into microscopic moulds. Unbearable odors surrounded them. Their hands and robes grew stiff with blood. And the things continued to be born. The things you saw in the grove, Mallare. There are hundreds of them already on the island."

"What are they?" I asked. "There was one that looked at me."

"They are bits of tissue pressed and warmed within moulds that glow with fires," Kora answered. "They take shape and the workers fondle them as if they were infants. They croon over these monsters. When they are newly out of the moulds they hold them in the palms of their hands and when the deformities begin to appear they shake their heads sadly. They no longer dismember the growths and search with luminous knives for the secrets within. Until last night there was a continual but futile improvement in the things that were born. Jacobi spoke to me. He has become almost as strange as these monsters he brings into the world. His body has withered. Blood seems to have gone out of him.

[119]

" 'We have perfected the moulds,' he said. 'The tissue plasms are accurately synthesized. Yet we hatch only teratisms. We produce the human alive with organs and arteries. But the figure is crippled always. Displacements and adhesions seem inevitable. And there is an unevenness about the growth we have not yet overcome. Some of the tissues devour the others. The arms feed on the head. Abnormalities result. But these we are slowly overcoming. He will be born soon.' "

Kora paused and shuddered.

"The God," she sighed, "the Thing out of nothing. I have left because I do not want to see it until it grows. It will come here as the others have. There is a curious impulse that animates these children of the hills. Each as it matures starts creeping over the stones toward the grove. For days they wander here, drawing closer to the Temple as if a magnet were pulling them. The door has been kept shut so they cannot enter and after a time they move away. They return to the stone hills. I have watched them with Jacobi at night, climbing tortuously until they reach the summit. Then they roll, emitting curious noises, into the sea. He looks at them and wrings his hands as they disappear and keeps whispering, 'they are alive.' Yes, Mallare, all these shapes you saw were living things. But until last night accidents corrupted them."

"What happened last night?" I whispered as she became silent.

"You will see," she answered softly, "the work is ended."

{12}

From the Journal of Mallare:—

Synthemus, the God, is in the Temple.
Weeks have passed and no one has dared enter
the place into which He walked. We have
heard His voice. It comes during the night in a
long, mournful roar. The sound is that of a
wounded beast.

Each time it has risen it has been louder.
For the last five nights He has cried out in a
bellow so tremendous and so mournful that we
who are forever gazing at the Temple fell to
our knees and covered our faces. All day there
is no sound from the Temple but the faint
thunder that rumbles ceaselessly up and down
its towering walls. But when darkness comes we
listen eagerly. The towers hover over the island
like gigantic and illumined flakes of snow. We
sit in Sebastien's house—all of us who were in
the caves—and wait. The old men cluster
around Sebastien, murmuring to him, their eyes

peering into the sky where the flower that blooms out of the Temple hangs like a black and distant island in space.

I wait beside Kora. She lies on her cushions and has not spoken for days. Her face is as expressionless as Sebastien's. She looks continually out of the window.

We know now when the sound will come. When the day lifts its invisible face in the night, when the shadows waver and the deep tremble of unseen light fills the silence—in this first fog of dawn He cries out. His voice like a cloud of sound hangs over the island, swelling and filling the night. For a time it seems that His cry will never end. It continues to mount until our senses, shaking with its noise, can no longer endure its ascent. It is at this moment when the ecstasy of the roar breaks and the bellow expires into a lingering and tormented droop of sound that our knees give way. Our God, hidden in the Temple, sobs as the dawn touches his eyes.

I move about among the workers asking questions. But they ignore me. At night I crouch at Kora's feet and remember His coming into the grove. It was the day following her talk of the monsters. She summoned me early and ordered me to come with her. The grove was empty. The monsters had disappeared. She led me to a place near the Temple door. Here in the green, dim air through which the heavy odors moved like paralyzed winds, we waited.

Sebastien appeared. He passed us without turning his eyes. We watched him open the door of the Temple and stand for a moment on its threshold.

"He is sad," I whispered to Kora. "He would like to occupy the Temple. He has dreamed of being its God and now he prepares the way for Another."

Kora frowned.

"It is not for him," she answered harshly. "Sebastien cannot even stand up inside the walls."

"Yet it is he who is our master," I argued. "It was Sebastien who brought us here, Sebastien who raised the towers, who worked in the minds of my companions, who caused the Temple to bloom."

"But he is not enough," Kora smiled, her eyes becoming cruel.

We heard voices in a far part of the grove.

"They are coming," she cried.

The voices drew nearer. And then walking alone He appeared. He was taller than Sebastien. His eyes were wide apart. His body was smooth as a woman's and glistened in the dim air of the grove as if it had been painted white.

"He has grown," Kora murmured, "last night he was no larger than a child. Look, how beautiful he is. Marbled and symmetrical. He does not look at us."

"Where does He come from?" I asked.

"He is a brother of those you saw in the grove yesterday. They made him."

I cried out as He passed us, His face averted.

"Look! He is growing."

I shrank from the door. He was standing on the threshold. Against the rumbling of the Temple I could see Him increase. He was expanding slowly, rising higher from the ground, his body glistening and symmetrical, moving into greater dimensions. With each breath His size increased.

"He will be unable to enter the door," Kora murmured.

But as she spoke He stepped inside. The grove was filled with figures. They came eagerly forward and crowded around the door. They were my companions of the caves but I could no longer recognize them. Bent, withered, their faces scarred and overgrown, they seemed to live only in their eyes. I watched them moving about like queer, excited children and chattering among themselves.

Bernhard, the philosopher, tugged at my arm.

"Life without soul is a dangerous thing," he muttered, "did you see it?"

Another of the withered ones joined in.

"Dangerous because it will live forever, eh?" he answered the philosopher. "What you call soul is the disease that eats the tissues of man. Synthemus is immortal. There are no thoughts in Him to carbonize His organs, no senses to wear out His membranes. He can neither see nor hear, smell nor feel, yet He lives."

One of the throng chattering around the door fell suddenly to his hands and knees and crawled inside the Temple. The talk ceased. We waited and after long minutes he emerged.

Kora hurried to him. As she helped him to his feet I recognized in this emaciated, witch-like figure, Jacobi the scientist.

"Go in and see Him," he babbled waving his hands toward his colleagues. "He is growing, growing. Vast, infinite. He keeps on growing. Sebastien is inside watching him grow. Yes, Sebastien who stole us away kneels before Him and calls Him God. Wait. He is only begun. I held Him in my hand when He came out of the mould. A little thing with eyes and limbs. An homonculus that breathed and moved. He was not like the others that came before Him. I could see that even when we watched Him under the lens."

The figures around the door broke into exclamations.

"He is not like the others!"

"He is perfect."

"He will never stop growing!"

"He is God," Kora spoke softly.

"Yes, Sebastien calls Him God," Jacobi babbled again. "But He is nothing more than a piece of tissue in the form of a man. In the tissue we have grafted organs, fibers, membranes.

Each fraction of Him lives by itself and grows. There is no center—no brain. It is not an animal nor a man, but a composium of tissues all put toegther, all growing by themselves and connected by a spinal cord that has no brain. Yet you saw how alive He seemed as He walked. You saw Him walk into the Temple."

"He is God," Kora repeated.

We moved away from the door. Jacobi clung to our side.

"A piece of matter that can utter no sounds," the old one laughed excitedly. "The noises they emit are nothing more than breath escaping. Ah, and you should see His heart. A tiny, rudimentary thing. There was no need for a heart because there is no blood in Him. Blood would stop His growth. Blood is the wound in which life expires. He is almost bloodless. He can move, breathe, grow, but there will never be a voice nor a soul nor even an instinct."

"What is He then?" I asked.

"He is a plant," Jacobi answered.

"He is God," Kora repeated. "I saw His eyes as He looked into the Temple."

"Yes, they all move toward the Temple," Jacobi continued, "you recall the others. It is a phenomenon which confused me at first. But the sap in the walls draws them. The life in the great stalk acts as a magnet on their tissues. And they are drawn to the door. Tomorrow we will visit Him."

We entered Sebastien's house. The workers followed us. All day they sat in groups babbling and arguing. Some insisted that unevenness would overtake the growth and Synthemus, as they called Him, would degenerate into another tumorous mass such as they had often rolled into the sea. Others declared that the heredity plasms in the tissue cells once functioning as they were now, would keep the growth intact and that however large Synthemus became His proportions would never vary. There was discussion too concerning His mobility.

To all this complicated talk I listened sorrowfully. For I began to understand out of it that He in the Temple was no more than an intricate mechanism of flesh and cells—a growth whose single impulse was to increase. I looked at Kora fearfully. She had expected a God and instead there had entered the Temple only this Thing whose mystery was no more than a multiplication of cells to which the scientists had given the ingenious and horrible exterior of a man.

Darkness came and the voices subsided. Sleep entered the room. I remained beside Kora staring at her cruel and preoccupied eyes. The night had almost gone when a strange noise drifted toward us. It was a cry—muffled and drawn. It wailed in the darkness and died away. It wakened the sleepers.

"What was that?" someone called.

"It came from the sea," a voice answered.

"No," said Kora, "it came from the Temple."

"Yes. Yes. From the Temple," voices cried.

Jacobi shuffled toward us.

"Synthemus has no voice," he announced in a high pitched tone. "There is nothing with which he can make sounds."

"It was not a voice," one of the old men interrupted. "It was the noise of His breath. He has grown huge and the air escapes violently from His lungs."

"No," Kora answered. "He cried out. You heard Him. It was a cry. Sebastien will come and tell us."

In the doorway lighted with dawn Sebastien had appeared. He stood swaying, his eyes closed.

"He has just come from the Temple," Kora said. "I will talk to him."

She left the couch and approached Sebastien. His waxen face turned to her for a moment and with a frown that seemed to darken the room, he gestured her away. Alone, he walked into the chamber in which he sleeps.

After this hour a confusion fell on the scientists. They babbled violently and waited each night for His voice. Now they are finally silent, wearied with arguments. And when the bellow rises from the Temple they fall frightened to their knees. We have not seen Sebastien again. And Julian too has been absent, hidden no doubt in our room overhead.

What strange thing is happening in the Temple we do not know. We are afraid to enter even the grove. Jacobi has attached himself to

Kora. During the day he sits whispering questions that bristle with Greek and Latin words. Occasionally he fastens gleaming eyes on me and mutters.

"The tissues have generated something. We gave it no voice. Something has grown into Synthemus."

Kora smiles at him and when he stares at her with glittering, apprehensive eyes she repeats slowly,

"He is God."

{13}

From the Journal of Mallare:—

Kora led me to the Temple. It was night.

"I am tired of this fear," she spoke as we moved toward the grove, "I desire to see our God. What harm can He do me if I have come to worship Him? He is lonely and cries out for us."

We halted beyond the flowers. Kora raised her hand and pointed.

"Something moves up there," she added. "Do you see it?"

"The wind is stirring the Temple blossom," I answered.

"There is no wind. Look."

I let my eyes climb the black and vanishing wall of the Temple. The great flower was moving against the sky as if a hand were gently shaking it.

"Of what are you afraid?" she asked imperiously as I stepped back from the grove.

"You are my slave. Nothing can harm you."

"I am not afraid," I answered, "but my mind shudders under these appalling shadows."

In the garden we were silent. When we came to the thundering walls Kora spoke.

"I am going inside, Mallare. Open the door for me."

The door opened.

"Wait for me," she cried and unfastening her girdle she flung her robe to the ground. Naked she crossed the threshold. She had not bidden me follow. I crouched on my knees outside, waiting. The night drummed upon the Temple walls. I grew lonely and afraid. What was this darkness around me and these strange things that hovered in the air? What lay beyond the black and menacing hills that circled the island? How curiously the figures of the caves had changed. Waiting beside the wall, I remembered the first coming of Sebastien. Who was he and why had he never spoken to me? Kora and Julian alone seemed aware of me. Now Julian had hidden himself and Kora was within the Temple and I was alone in this crazed garden.

Suddenly as I crouched dreaming of my loneliness, screams burst from the door. One after another they came, frenzied and shattered sounds. I heard my name cried in terror. It was Kora screaming in a voice I had never heard. I crept into the Temple, trembling and bewildered.

The screaming ended. I lay with my face to the earth blinded by the glare that hammered against the walls. Slowly I raised my eyes and saw His feet standing in the midst of the white space. They were like two hills of flesh. Above them his legs loomed like white towers. Curve upon curve of flesh, billowing monstrous sails of flesh rose in an incalculable form amid the roar of the white walls. As my eyes ascended the mountainous body it began to move. I closed my eyes.

This was Synthemus, grown so vast He could no longer be understood; a swollen and gigantic burst of flesh whose outlines escaped the eye. The rumble of his breathing vied with the thunder of the walls. I could feel him moving over me and a hot wind beat in gusts upon my skin.

[137]

"His face," Kora was shouting, "have you seen His face? It is you. It is Mallare."

I remained with my eyes closed. As she spoke I remembered the thing in the garden that had turned to me. Staring out of the sack-like growth I had seen my face. The eyes and features of Mallare had looked at me out of an unholy mirror.

"They were all Mallares," I thought, growing faint, "each of these crawling and horrible shapes contained my face in them. Mallare looked out of all of them. It was I inside those foul bags of life."

"Look up," Kora commanded, "higher, to where His eyes shine."

I would look up and see myself again. But something would happen if I raised my eyes to this overwhelming image. These curving and formless walls of flesh were the legs of Mallare. I lifted my head. Slowly the colossus took shape. I beheld His thighs and arms and His tremendous field of sex; His torso and neck. And gazing down on me I saw His face, a white and enormous expanse of flesh in which two black fires glowed.

I crept closer to the wall. There was a mystery in this island I could no longer understand. It was I who lay huddled on the ground, I who knew myself for Mallare. What other Mallare was there? Ah, they play games with me. They bury me within tumorous and dreadful shapes that crawl through the garden and tumble down the stone hills into the sea. And now they transform me into an inflated, inconceivable monster imprisoned within the walls of the Temple and bellowing at night. This is Sebastien's doing. He plays with me. He amuses himself with my terror.

"This God is not Mallare," I thought. "It is someone else. I must be careful or I will see my face everywhere. Kora, Julian, the hermaphrodites, the workers in the hills and even Sebastien—yes, they will all assume my face as this God has done and I will dissolve in a mirror. I must cling to myself. Ah, what is there to remember? I was stolen in the fog. An evil and waxen creature lifted me away. The world vanished in a white cloud. And now there is left only this island on which a God grows."

I looked up. Kora was dancing, her body bending into slow postures, her arms twisting like serpents over her head. A confusion filled me. I felt myself changing. The thing I had dreaded was happening. I was dwindling, disappearing.

"I am vanishing," I murmured. "I will cease to be."

I became a tiny figure, a little thing too small to be seen. The noises in the Temple faded to whisps of sound. With my eyes that had narrowed to pin points I could see myself—a fragile, dwindling creature already no higher than an ant. Terrified, I realized that this speck crawling along the wall was I; that within its microscopic limbs Mallare was moving and breathing.

"It is Sebastien," I cried, "he is taking me away; erasing me as I once dreamed he would."

For moments during which my mind darkened it seemed that I no longer existed. My body was a smoke that had vanished. Then opening my eyes I saw myself, an amazing and delicate little seed of a man small enough to drown in a drop of water, yet complete and moving with infinitesimal legs over the ground.

"Ah," I thought furtively, "I still persist."

Slowly the mystery came to me. It was but a delusion. I had looked on the white and collosal face of this thing in the Temple and my eyes had lost their reason. A Mallare so enormous had gazed down on me that I had vanished in the comparison. Yes, in the garden my dimensions would return.

I heard Kora's voice above the noises. No longer frightened by my tininess I looked around until I saw her. She was standing with her arms lifted. A chant came from her lips. I listened to the tinkle of faraway words without moving.

"Oh God," she spoke, "who rises high in the Temple, raise me to your lips. Let me warm your lips with my body. I am Kora whose body is a sob of pleasure, whose soul is a mist that wanders through a delirium in quest of life. I am Kora at whose touch flesh blooms with mysteries; in whose arms men ride across Hells. Oh God who stares at me from the Temple height raise me in your hand and I will walk like a deep kiss into your soul. I will shatter myself in your mouth and pour dreams into your veins. I am weary of the night in which I live, of the shadows that feed on my caresses. I am weary of the dreams that embrace me, of the phantoms that borrow their cries from me, I am tired of my hunger. I am sick with the couches on which I lie. Let me find peace in you. Devour me and I will become a little earthly servant within the halls of your body. Let me kiss you and die. ."

The chant ended and I saw the God move. He was sinking to His knees. A field of flesh filled the Temple. His hands hovered like great clouds over the ground. A finger and thumb that could have crushed the stone hills between them closed around Kora. Held within this gigantic embrace as if she were an insect, He lifted her up.

"She is gone," I thought. "His hand has closed on her."

I called her name. A commotion filled the Temple. Its walls were shaking and the earth lifted around me. The God was on His knees, His hands beating at the Temple sides. Under the blows they shook as if they would burst apart. His head was thrown back and out of the

cavernous mouth issued a roar that repeated itself in a continual crescendo. His hands smiting
blindly at the walls, a torment, thunderous and
deafening soared out of Him. And in the bellow
of His voice lay a human note—a bewildered
and rapacious cry such as desire wrings out of
flesh, such as lust tears from the soul.

The air in the Temple grew hot. The wall
against which I crouched seemed to burn. I saw
Kora again, a figure flying and stumbling up a
hill of flesh. Waving her arms she raced on the
thigh of the God. Faraway I saw her fall and
lie still. Then motionless she began to rise in
space. The walls of the Temple rattled as if a
wind were uprooting them. His cries swept
down upon me like a storm. High above I
caught a glimpse of Kora crawling on her hands
and knees. I saw her straighten and with her
arms outstretched and her mouth opened in a
laugh I could no longer hear, stand on the crest
of a burning hill. Then slowly she began to disappear.

I rushed out of the door. In the grove I lay
on the ground unable to bear the noises bursting
from the Temple. The earth about me was shak-

ing and the great stalk was swaying in the darkness.

"His hands will uproot the walls," I thought. "It will come down. The island will be torn to pieces."

Bestial and hideous, the roars increased. Ah, it was for this His loneliness had bellowed in the dawn. They had created Him to grow like a plant of flesh, bloodless and inviolable. But a voice had taken form in Him. A voice had come from nowhere and was crying now in the night filling the island with a tumult of despair and ecstasy. The roots of the Temple were straining at the earth. For the moment there came to me a vision of the white and enormous face stamped with agony. The eyes that had gazed down at me from the Temple summit were closed. The billowing, monstrous sails of flesh were thrashing against the white walls. A soul, raging and hungering, was taking birth within his veins.

Suddenly the sounds of torment ceased and the Temple grew still. The dark grove was filled with an overpowering alkaline odor. Around me the towering stems began to glisten.

A thick and unnatural rain was descending—an opalescent deluge that glimmered with light, that crept over the ground in heavy and phosphorescent pools. I stood up and began to run. But everywhere the flood gathered until I floundered through a swamp that sucked at my feet and tumbled me into its warm and glistening surface. Engulfed and suffocating I crawled on until I came to the figure of Kora lying face downward, inert and half hidden. I lifted her in my arms and stumbled into the open night.

Here I laid her down. Her naked body was lifeless and glittering.

"Kora," I cried, "It is I, Mallare. Open your eyes."

I fell beside her and wept, repeating her name through my tears. At last I saw her move.

"I am dying," she whispered.

A fear overcame me.

"Yes, let me die," she spoke. "You will remember me with beautiful words."

"Sebastien," I muttered.

"You are his slave, Mallare," she answered softly, "You will tell him I found no sleeping place within the God, that I have flown through the night and that I lie crushed and spent outside the garden. He will weep. Perhaps even he will wander off and then, Mallare, you will escape. I am weary of his cruel embraces. He is like a whip twisting around me. Each night he whispers to me of the new marvels he will bring forth if I caress him."

I clung to her hands as she spoke.

"Ah, you will not let me die, poor slave," she murmured. "You return me to life."

"To Sebastien," I sighed.

The hermaphrodites surrounded us. They lifted her from the ground. I lay and watched them taking her into the darkness. The night had grown cold. Standing near me was Sebastien. His head was raised to the Temple summit. A silence had fallen. He ignored me when I called his name. I crept to his feet and crouched beside him. For a long time he stood motionless. Then his head sank and he covered his face with his arm.

{14}

From the Journal of Mallare:—

I am lonely and bewildered. An unhappiness has fallen over the Kingdom. The bellowing of the God has resumed. His cries begin in the darkness and last until light comes.

They have built an instrument in the stone hills, hollowing out the highest of them into thousands of pipes. The sea and wind moving against the hill convert it into a great stone organ out of which rises a crashing and disheveled music. Day and night there is a boom and screech of chords over the hills. The stone pipes sigh and scream and shake out a continuous cannonade of basses; release sudden obligatoes that burst like sky rockets inside one's ears. These sounds when I first heard them seemed only a furious din. But gradually the monotonous tumult has become a song—a hymn beating endlessly out of the sky.

I have explained to Julian that what we hear is the mournful and intimate melody of

nature magnified through the stone throats of
the hill. But he looks at me with frowning eyes.
His smile does not return. I find him always
sitting in the corner of our room and when I
talk he regards me with a crazed and melancholy stare.

It is Kora who has brought the disquietude.
Since the night I carried her out of the flooded
garden she has lain most of the time on her
couch without moving. She ignores those who
come near her. The room has grown sultry.
The air is difficult to breathe. She lies heavy
lidded and silent until night comes. When the
room grows dark she rises from her couch and
walks to the door behind which Sebastien waits.

One strange thing has happened. Women
have arrived in the Kingdom. Out of the window I watched them passing through the streets.
They were nude and came from different lands.
Slow moving, sinuous women with tropical eyes,
dark skins and long breasts; voluptuous, flaxen
women whose flesh is heavy and soft; slender
women with silken bodies and vaporous hair—
one by one they disappeared into the towers.
They have mounted to the rooms and stretched

themselves upon innumerable couches. Here they lie with strange smiles on their faces, grimacing langorously, moving faintly like a swarm of wanton butterflies imprisoned within the crystaline towers.

After I had watched them passing through the streets I arose one morning determined to find out the mystery of their presence in the Kingdom. The procession had ended. The towers were filled. All day I spent climbing the twisting stairways that lead from room to room. I beheld black, barbaric women whose mouths opened in sudden laughters at the sight of me and who turned on their beds in ritulastic postures. Others, yellow skinned and ebony haired, doubled their bodies into snail-like arcs and fluttered their fingers as I passed. Others arranged their milk white torsoes in intimate and lascivious poses. Some lay like nuns with their eyes closed and their hands on their breasts. Some twisted like hungry serpents among the cushions.

I grew sickened as I moved through the rooms. An incompleted Saturnalia filled the towers. I saw that some had gilded their bodies and that some had painted their breasts and cheeks and that others had hung themselves with ornaments so that their thighs glittered and their hair shone like lanterns. Nuns and Messalinas, virgins and houris, they sprawled nude and multitudinous about me. Decorated with paints and gems, their eyes swimming in lecherous dreams they lay upon the thousands of couches exhaling the perfumes of lust. Each as I passed made her sign to me. Some moaned, others laughed harshly; some grimaced, twitching their shoulders and pouting their lips, others closed their eyes and extended their arms; some flung themselves into disgusting postures, others rose to their knees as if in prayer and rolled their eyes upward.

Toward night I hurried back to Kora and dropped exhausted at her feet.

"A plague of women has descended on the island," I spoke to her. "Sebastien has brought them here and they lie waiting for him. They stretch themselves on the couches amid ornaments and cries. They writhe and laugh and an insatiable hunger lights their eyes. They have come from cities and fields and jungles and are covered with curious jewels and wear strange

head dresses. There are madonnas and virgins, creatures with the faces of saints, with the eyes of sleepy children, with the cold lips of nuns. There are odalisques with amber colored breasts and queens whose skins are white as the bellies of frogs. There are barbaric nymphs whose bodies are smooth as black drums and proud women and wantons and creatures who posture like the engravings on ancient temple walls. I walked among them until my head grew dizzy. The towers have become like odorous and noisy butcher shops. For what purpose has Sebastien brought them?"

"I do not know," Kora answered harshly.

"Of what use are women in our Kingdom?" I continued. "Their bodies writhing and lecherous conceal an identical platitude. Perhaps they are to dance in the Temple."

"They are of no use," Kora spoke. "Sebastien is a fool. I am sick of this prison in which he keeps me. I dream of invisible things and he peoples our island with towers and strumpets. At night he whispers to me that the Kingdom is mine, that he creates it daily for me. He promises me new diversions. Out of his mind he hatches miracles and novelties. Yes, his mind can create all things but those I desire. I desire something that does not exist on this island."

She arose and stretched her body. Her eyes, heavy and sullen, frowned over me.

"There is something else," she murmured, "something that pulls me away as if heavy hands were lifting my body. I have asked him for my desire. He brought God into the Temple and for a time as I listened to His cry in the dawn I believed that here at last in this kingdom hemmed by fevers and deleriums, an infinite One had taken form. There is a shape, a thing, a light, a sound toward which I turn. Yet it is nowhere in the Kingdom. What I desire is not here. It is not in the God who fills the Temple. Sebastien has deceived me again. This God is no more than another image of himself—a gigantic and groaning satyr. I am bruised and sickened, Mallare. He has prisoned me in this Kingdom and all his miracles are phantom bars against which I strain and expire."

{15}

From the Journal of Mallare:—

As I slept at the foot of her couch I felt her stir. She arose and bending over me made certain I had not heard her. Then she walked slowly from the room.

When she had disappeared I sprang to my feet and followed her cautiously. This was the third time she had gone on her nocturnal visit. Each time fear had withheld me. But on this night the desire to learn her secret led me through the dark room.

Outside the house I saw her moving toward the garden. I crept after her in the shadows. In the distance I saw Julian standing at the edge of the grove that surrounds the Temple. I hid myself as they came together. For a time their voices were low. Then suddenly I heard Julian, grown angry, cry out,

"Leave me. There is only madness in your embrace."

Kora's voice answered,

"I am dying, Julian. Hold me for a moment. Life returns to me when I feel your breath upon me."

Again there was silence and I hid myself deeper in the shadows. The darkness, heavy with the odor of flowers, filled the garden with tunnels. Above the rumbling of the Temple walls came the wail of the God and out of the stone throats in the hills arose deep and mournful sounds.

The two moved towards the edge of the grove and stood facing the towers from whose crystaline walls an opal light glittered. I understood now the change that had overtaken my grinning and contemptuous friend. He had not spoken to me since the night I had carried Kora out of the flooded garden. It was apparent now. This crazed and ridiculous poet had fallen in love with Kora. She had finally penetrated the delusions which surround him.

"It is madness even to talk to you," he resumed after a long silence. "Why do you come to me? Do you fancy I too am like the shadows in which you foul yourself?"

"You are still angry," she answered.

"No. I am sick," Julian frowned. "I am no longer sane. Knowing who you are I yet speak to you."

"Who am I, Julian," she asked.

"Am I less mad than he, now? I keep a rendezvous with you in this evil garden," he continued. "I talk to you as if you were a woman, as if this body you uncover for me were real. Yet even as you breathe upon me and I feel the warmth of your thighs, I know the hideous secret of your existence."

"There are many secrets in the night," Kora spoke. "Let the darkness hide them. You alone hold what I desire."

"What you desire," Julian repeated, "you wander through the night desiring something. Yes, I know who you are. You are the lust that lives in Mallare and to which his madness has given a body. Like an allegorical figure of Passion you occupy the pantomime of his mania. And I, too, who am awake—I stumble through the cruel dream with which he surrounds himself. Since I have come to this place I have smiled unwaveringly at illusion. I have not been deceived. And I tell you again, it is all mist, all shadow. There is no island, no kingdom. There is only the broken and glittering mind of Mallare."

I waited for her to laugh at this madman in the garden. I could see him standing and frowning pompously at the night. His face that had once been beautiful and gentle looked wildly into the shadows. But she made no sound. Her body remained curved in adoration before him, her face lifted to his babbling.

"The dream has grown too intricate," he resumed. "My eyes and hands do not distinguish between you and me. You whom I know for a shadow seem made of the same substance as I."

"What difference do your thoughts make, Julian?" she cried. "What does it matter if we are real or not? Who is there to judge but ourselves? Why must you question? Here is night and the odor of flowers. And if I am beautiful to your eyes why must your thought distort me with meanings?"

"You stand and plead with me," Julian continued. "There is some mystery about this that avoids me. You are not as innocent of it as your words."

"Let me caress you," she murmured.

"It comes to me," he drew back from her. "I am like yourself—a shadow. Until I saw you following me with amorous eyes I thought myself real. So little is required to convince a man that he lives."

A laugh, bitter and despairing, came from him and he turned his crazed eyes upon Kora.

"Who in this Kingdom is more mad than I?" he cried, "I, who existing amid shadows fancied myself alive. And now a shadow lusts after me. A thing that has no being pleads with me for love. He came to me at night and whispered, 'Kora desires you.' Ah, this cunning and involved Mallare. You are his passion, Kora; his senses masquerading in the clothes of life. Did I not see in your face even at the first moment the features of Mallare? You are the phantom risen from his veins, the mystery of his senses he has called Kora. And he has established you as the queen at whose feet he brings his madness as a gift."

I shuddered in the darkness as I heard her answer.

[159]

"You speak always of Mallare. He is repulsive to me. I have made him my slave. He lies at my feet not daring to touch me."

"You withhold yourself," Julian frowned, "because there is an incestuous touch to his embrace. You make him your slave. And Mallare, the slave of his senses, is happy. He joins the hermaphrodites who serve you. He is pleased to be one with these strange phantoms he has created and whose double bodies are the ugly symbols of his self love."

"Look how black the night is," Kora whispered. "I am at your feet, Julian. There is no one in the garden but us."

Again the poet's voice grew wild. I could see his hands seizing his head and his fingers pressing despairingly against his face. I smiled at the torment of his gesture.

"We stand in these shadows and talk," he cried, "and I listen knowing there are no sounds, knowing there is no garden, no figures. We are the hallucinations of Mallare, puppets grown egoistic and garrulous. I see everything that happens in this delirium. I see the fever out of which the towers were born, out of which everything about us has taken form. I see you—the mystery in the veins of Mallare, the dark and tumultuous one whose voice sings in his head. He gives you the form of a woman and pursues you through his dream, whispering to himself that in your kiss he will find the deep and secret ecstacy he desires. Towers, Temples, Gods, couches alive with writhing women, miracles of sound and gesture—in the midst of these hallucinations I remain faithful to life, untouched by dreams. I know that what I see is a mist in the head of Mallare. But, ah, I see myself. I hear myself talk. I stand here, caressing you. And I know by this that I, too, am a fantasy. For there is no I. Were I not mad I would know this. I would know that I am the Mallare who lingers in an undarkened corner watching the debacle of himself. But no. His madness is so powerful that it has made a phantom even of his lingering sanity. It has given me a shape and voice and with the rest of you I wander over the island proclaiming myself a part of this dream."

His crazed voice broke and his hands seized her. Never have I seen anyone so mad, nor heard words so heavy with anguish as came from him in the shadows of the garden.

"Listen," he cried. "It is Mallare who holds you. Look at my face. Is it not his? Whose voice do you hear now? Tell me I am Mallare and I will love you."

"No, it is you, Julian," Kora answered. "Mallare is repulsive to me. I can give him only blows. In his presence a nausea and loneliness consume me. Why must you ask questions when it is so dark? Of what use are the answers? Come lie beside me. I desire you."

"Mallare is repulsive to you," Julian again drew away from her, "yet you are his bride. You have gone to him each night in the room beyond the couches."

"There is no one there but Sebastien," Kora spoke.

"Sebastien," Julian repeated. "And who is Sebastien? Who rules us? Who fills the air with monsters? Have you not looked closely at his face. Sebastien is the treasured and mysterious thing Mallare once called his mind. When you lie in the arms of this phantom a grewsome wedding is enacted. Mallare consummates the union of his senses and his thought. Yes, he deceives you. And when you grow weary of this deception and ask for a God—for one beyond Mallare, for strange lips to touch, for hands that will thrust themselves out of another world—he deceives you again. The God in the Temple is but another Mallare. You turn in disgust from this cunning and involved slave. But betray him with whatever figures come into this island and your lips raised to the new lover will touch only the lips of Mallare."

"Take me away, Julian," she cried suddenly, "it is true."

"So you have known that," he answered.

"Yes," I heard her say and in the silence that fell I tried to step from the shadows which hid me. A rage toward this ranting and ridiculous poet had come into my head. But I was unable to move. I felt myself sinking to the ground as if a spell were upon me. And suddenly through the horror which gripped my senses I knew Sebastien was standing near, that he had come into the garden and, hidden in the darkness he was listening like myself to the voices.

"I have known all you have said," Kora continued. "And since I saw you I have dreamed of only one thing—to escape."

"There is no other night for us but this black mirage his fever spreads," Julian answered. "What escape is there for one who is but an illusion? How can we break from this evil Kingdom in which we seem to live? This island is no more than the head of Mallare ruled by his madness that moves like a waxen, expressionless monster behind our days. And how escape the head of Mallare? If I escape whom do I take with me? What existence is there for me outside this dream in which I am mad enough to fancy myself alive? I have sat for months smiling at Mallare and wondering which of us was the hallucination of the other. Now I understand and I am afraid. If I escape it will be he who will remain. I am nothing more than the irreconcilable phantom of his sanity. I have taken form in the undarkened corner of his brain. Like an interloper I move across this delirious and fantastic stage, staring at its hideous fictions with the eyes of life."

"But what difference is all this?" Kora cried. "What more meaning is there to life than

this? Mallare has fallen to pieces. We are the fragments with which a mystery diverts itself. Lie beside me. Let me hear you talk. There is nothing else but our bodies in the night. Why must we dream of worlds that do not exist when a garden surrounds us?"

"Yes, a garden," said Julian and sank to the earth beside her. "You seem almost beautiful as you talk. It is not from you I turn. But my eyes are sickened of this land and all that is part of it. These towers and the erotic images that moan and gesture within them, the Temple and its bellowing God—all the visions and tumults of this Kingdom are the furniture of a fever that sickens me. I am sick of this fever. Day upon day as I lie imprisoned in this valley I remember the world beyond these stone hills—the white days that fell from the sun. Ah, what a dismal and sickly substitute for life Mallare's Kingdom is. How wretched these phantoms seem beside those other and majestic images I once knew—the vast and silent sky, the black walls of night."

"Was that not a dream too?" Kora spoke.

[167]

"Yes," he answered, "all that too was a phantom—the beautiful and skillful dream of life. It haunts me amid the shadows of this island. I am part of this other dream, a fantasy so fresh and infinite that its memory is like a flower dying in my heart. It is for this dream I long, Kora—I sit staring at a vanished world that lies somewhere beyond this venereal pantomime in which we are captive. I long for life. In this dream that has disappeared there were winds blowing out of nowhere, there were streets and skies and faces and beyond them a halo of myths and mathematics. And I was Mallare. I was part of Mallare. He is gone now and I am all that remains of him, a reluctant shadow moving within his madness. We all lived in Mallare, all these towers and monsters and great noises. Ah, I remember him, I am in love with him. His senses were gardens through which he wandered smiling. There was a mystery that sometimes touched his soul till he became conscious of a stranger peering out of his eyes and beholding things that had no existence. This was Mallare—a smiling and lonely bit of life;

[168]

a startling adjective in an interminable and monotonous sentence whose meaning was lost to itself.

"How can I love in this land when my soul is sick with the nostalgia for other scenes. I remember another dream in which Mallare lived. I remember him tall, proud and smiling with his hair in a black slant above his eyes. Around him were the sadness and emptiness of life—the vast and lonely hall in whose corner man strikes his tiny posture of bewilderment. Here in this corner was a noise and violence. Here Mallare wept and spat and laughed. And wearied of the din he would raise his eyes, and an illusion, beautiful and infinite, made love to him. Sky, wind and darkness—these were part of an endless dream. Ships moving over the sea, insects crawling over blades of grass, the voices of men and winds; blood and odors and the leaves of trees, the avalanche of night and the flying gardens of day—around him whispering its strange language life emptied its dream. It rose out of an unknown sleep. Glittering and vast it spread itself in tremendous decorations, it offered itself in mysterious disguises. And staring too long into its mystic face Mallare grew sick. He spoke to himself, 'there is a dream in the mind of man more beautiful and strange than the phantom his senses have inherited. An inner world, an existence within the walls of thought!'

"He desired this—to be free of life, to crawl out of the mystery which held him. And here it is—this crude and capricious mirage we inhabit—here is the little sexual nightmare man calls his soul. Here are its phallic mansions, its skies of semen, its fever rotted music and lecherous mirrors."

The crazed words ended. Frightened I clung to the earth waiting for the sight of Sebastien. He would step out and his eyes would destroy the mad poet. The babbler would fall to his knees, weeping with terror. But Sebastien still remained hidden. I watched Julian arise.

"Mallare," he cried, "see what you have done. Out of thought you have created everything but thought. I am all that thinks in your Kingdom, I, the image out of another dream, and I too grow mad. There will be nothing left when I go, nothing but flashes and sounds. An inferno out of which reason has vanished will devour itself in torments."

Shaking his arms over his head he stood looking down at Kora. She arose and as if fearful of him, pressed herself upon his body.

"We are dying here," she spoke. "There is some way to go from here."

"None," he answered.

"Let us find an escape," Kora repeated. "Let us climb the hills and throw ourselves into the sea."

"There is no door out of this Kingdom," Julian replied. "We have existence only within these hills. Beyond them there is no earth to hold us. We will vanish. He will be left without us."

"What difference," Kora cried. "Let him remain."

She seized his hand.

"Come," she drew him forward, "I know the way through the hills."

They began to walk and Sebastien stepped out of the shadows and confronted them. Julian halted and stood staring at the waxen figure in the night. Kora, covering her face, crouched behind her lover.

"Ah, my glowering maniac," Julian shouted suddenly, "you have come for her, eh? There he is Kora. Stand up and look at him. There is the real Mallare. The rest of us are shadows moving in his veins. He has come for his bride. Look, she crawls back to his feet. Return to him then. I go alone. Mad—yes, I am more mad than you, Sebastien. Come, follow me. Try to drag me back. I will climb these hills and escape into the sea beyond them."

There was a silence during which Kora, clinging to the figure of Sebastien wept and hid her face. At this moment when I cowered waiting for Sebastien's wrath to strike and shatter the scene around me, I became aware that a strange thing was happening. Julian was escaping. Walking slowly and waving his arms he was crying in a crazed and melancholy voice,

"Farewell, Mallare. Not to your towers and phantoms but to you. Farewell."

He was gone. I sprang to my feet and pointed my finger at Sebastien.

[172]

"You have let him escape," I cried. "Go, follow him. Drag him back. We will lift him to the jaws of the God and destroy him."

Sebastien turned his malignant eyes on me. There is a power in his eyes that undresses me of myself. But this time although I felt myself swaying and vanishing as if a death were slowly obliterating me, I stood before him and struggled to speak. For moments I could make no sound. Then suddenly irresistible words sprang from the sleep overcoming me.

"I am not your slave. I am not afraid of you," I heard myself shouting, "I will follow Julian and escape with him. You are no longer King. He laughed at you. And I too laugh."

What followed I do not remember. I do not remember whether he spoke to me. I heard Julian's laugh float out of the night. In this moment, enraged by the weakness of Sebastien, I turned and sought to move away. But Sebastien lifted his hand to destroy me and I fell screaming across the motionless body of Kora.

{16}

From the Journal of Mallare:—

I am to be sacrificed. Fires are burning in the Temple. At night the island is filled with the hill music, the ceaseless bellowing of the God and the shrill cries of women. The walls of the room in which they have imprisoned me shake with the noises.

Through the window I can see the women in the streets. They run among the towers at night waving torches over their heads. The broken light of the flames covers their bodies with fluttering red shawls. They leap as they run and at each bellow from the Temple their voices rise in a chorus of screams.

As the night grows deeper they indulge in wild antics. Leaving the towers they approach the temple garden and with their torches blazing circle the grove. Some of them while running stiffen suddenly in their delirium and squat, feet apart, bodies thrust forward and heads raised

in postures of inanimate and bestial ecstasy.
Others sit on the ground their legs outstretched
and howl as the runners pass. Until dawn the
race of the women around the Temple continues. In the last moments of darkness when the
voice of the God rises in a continuous roar, the
naked figures begin to leap with the frenzy that
precedes exhaustion. They belabor each other
with the burning torches. They trample one another to the ground and lie writhing in glistening mounds of flesh, clawing, screeching, blood
flowing from their mouths and nails.

Dawn comes. The carnival ends with the
light. They rise and with their torches paled
by the sun walk drunkenly back to the towers.
The secret of these nocturnal scenes grows apparent to me. They are waiting for the night
when the door of the Temple will open for
them. The voice of the God has crazed their
bodies. They are swollen and diseased with lust.
On the night in which I am killed they will
swarm into the Temple and embrace the God.

I have thought of my death and found it
curious. There will be something very strange
about my death. As I wait for the moment in

which I am to end a sense of deception fills me.
Something inconceivable is to occur. Why am
I not afraid of death and why does my thought
remain amused by the doom Sebastien has pro-
nounced upon me? I do not believe in death.
Yet not to believe in death is to pretend that one
is not alive. In the world from which I was
stolen there was life and death. The scene alone
was immortal; man came and went. Here in
the Kingdom it is only the scene that can die.
It is unwise to think of things or I will become
like Julian. Let the night of my death come.
I will sit and amuse myself with memories and
conjectures. In the world beyond the stone hills,
if that still exists, life is the intangible accident
from whose everlasting moment a fantasy rises.
Man emerges from this invisible and accidental
shell of spirit and runs with a debacle at his
heels. In that world life pursues its little frag-
ment in him, reaching with inexorable hands for
the illusion he calls his soul. Like a thief who
has snatched a lantern from the road, man runs,
swinging his borrowed and mysterious light
through the dark, and in its fugitive gleam
searching futiley for a hiding place. This is his

day in that world—a thief hunted by nature. See what becomes of him when he dies. He lies motionless and empty, his body lingers for a moment like a discarded mistake—and the lantern gleams move on. Between the closing of his eyes and his death an eternity which neither time nor thought can measure separates him and the lantern gleams.

But this death that awaits me in the Temple where the fires are burning is a dissolution stranger and more subtle than the death of man. I must not resist it. For what difference does it make? The Kingdom will remain. Kora and Sebastien and the figures that move among the wonders of the island will continue. These things of which I am an indissoluable part will live on. Yes, if I die there will be a Mallare without Mallare to know him.

What was this babbling of Julian that remains in my thought? In the beginning there were ideas in my head. There was meaning to the mysteries around me. But now I am no longer Mallare, but a likeness of Mallare that survives in a dream. The dreamer will continue. Only a phantom of which he has tired will vanish. How cold sorrow is. I sit before my window and say farewell—to whom? My vanishing will be unimportant. Yes, it is forbidden me to think. They will come for me soon. I have not answered questions in my head. Why does the God who bellows wear the face of Mallare? And the things in the garden I saw with Julian. Ah, I cannot understand this yet it persists in my mind. It persists that my death will make no difference. I am not I. I am somewhere else. Sorrow and fear confuse me. My thoughts ride away upon winds. But this death of Mallare is an illusion. They are coming into the streets again, running and screaming. I will think of nothing. I will sit pretending there is no Mallare. And I will hear him walking up the steps. Let him take me and destroy me. I am not Mallare. I have deceived him from the beginning. When his hands seize me I will close my eyes. I will watch from somewhere, from beyond the hills perhaps. Hey, Sebastien! Open the doors. There is someone who sits before a window waiting for you. Take him away.

[17]

From the Journal of Mallare:—

The army stands on the hills. Piltendorff is taller than the rest. Brown and shaggy he runs hither and thither and leaps into the air, his knees lifted, his arms outspread like a jumping jack.

It is day and the army still covers the hills. Its trumpets blow valiently, its soldiers flatten themselves on the rocks and peer down into the valley. But despite the jumping up and down of Piltendorff and the heralding of his trumpets the army refuses to advance.

It has been on the hills since night. It came after they had carried me into the Temple. When I was about to die the hill music suddenly ended and trumpets blew in the night.

Earlier, when darkness began, they had placed me in a bowl made of gold and the hermaphrodites bore me across the valley. As we moved the women came running and screaming out of the towers. I lay in the huge bowl and stared over its rim at the starless sky. As we drew nearer to the grove the voices of the women became wilder. With their torches waving, their faces contorted and reddened they leaped into the air around me. Beholding me crouched in the bowl bottom they screeched and disappeared and the procession continued.

We passed through the garden in an increasing uproar. I saw the bodies of women climbing the bending flower trunks. They hurled their torches hilariously into the air and vaulted like white breasted apes over the bowl. The odor of their bodies frightened me. I closed my eyes as we entered the Temple.

Great bon fires were burning in a circle of caldrons. The flames drummed and crackled and their glare reddened the walls. The God, crouching on His knees filled the circle with his monstrous shape. I saw Sebastien standing on a platform high above the ground. His face was dark and glowering. Beside him stood Kora dressed in her red robe and holding a serpent in her hand. She was pale and her eyes as they turned to me were filled with sleep.

The bellowing of the God began and all other sounds were crushed in my ears. I hid in the bowl as the tumult increased and after a long time I felt myself rising. I was being lifted slowly through the Temple space. I looked over the rim and saw the women bodies, as I had once seen Kora, racing over the flesh of the Monster. Hundreds upon hundreds of naked figures were swarming upon his thighs, mounting to his hips and arms. They covered him in a moving veil of flesh. In my ascent I passed swarms of them screeching and flattened against His body. They beat with their hands and feet upon the God and rolled over and over in a voluptuous frenzy. I beheld others in the distance become like little clusters of white insects clinging to the towering walls of His flesh.

I continued to mount. Kora and Sebastien were far beneath me and the fires on the floor of the Temple had dwindled to red discs. I realized slowly that I was in His hand, that they had placed the golden bowl in the midst of His palm and that He was raising it to his lips. I stood up and waved my arms in terror but the ascent continued.

He was to devour me. It was for this the fires had been kindled and the women were dancing in the abyss below. I struggled out of the bowl and found myself on a tremendous platform. Hidden torrents swept under my feet. In the distance I could see His fingers rising as he sought to curl them over me. I fled and the ascent grew swifter. The nails of His fingers hovered like opal cliffs over my head. Arrived at the edge of His hand I threw myself down and peered into the Temple depths.

The fires below were like flickering match flames. Nothing more was to be seen. A cylindrical abyss pulled at my eyes and covering my face I struggled erect.

His breath fell on me and I saw He was moving me toward the cavern of His mouth. He had risen to His feet and thrust His head through the Temple roof. The odor of the gigantic blossom through which I was lifted began to overcome me. The night was lighted only by His eyes. The hill music filled the darkness with faint and trembling sounds. We were outside the Temple and I had closed my eyes, almost dead with the blows of His breath upon me

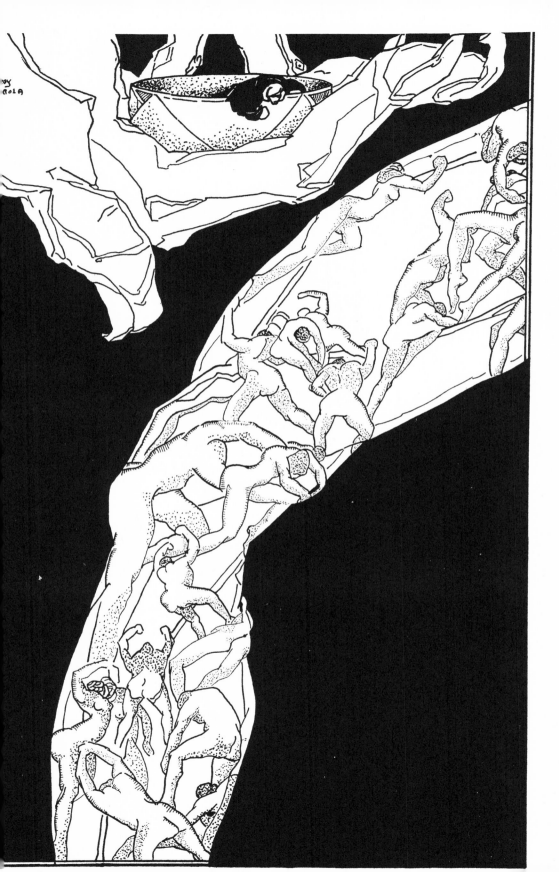

and the roaring of the air into His body, when
the music ended. There was a pause and I heard
a trumpet blow far away. The great head above
me lifted and a moment later a bellow that
stunned all my senses rolled from His mouth.

When I opened my eyes again the hand in
which I lay had grown wet. An arrow was protruding from the forehead of the God—a huge,
imbedded shaft. Streams of blood were running
down His face. The hand grew flooded and
struggling to stand I was swept down. For a
long time I slid and tumbled down the wall of
His body, until I found myself in the midst of
the clusters of naked figures. Here I rested
watching the undiminished frenzy of the women
until the blood overtook us. The slow flood up-
rooted the figures and we slid and tumbled in its
depths. Some of them washed from the body
dropped suddenly through the air. Others
caught in the crevise of his thigh lay exhausted
and the blood flowed over them, hiding them.

The floor of the Temple was wet and odorous as I fell face downward from His body. The
fires were still burning. Crawling toward the
door I looked around me. Neither Sebastien

nor Kora was to be seen. At the door I staggered upright. The blood was moving in slow rivers down the towering walls of flesh. It rose around my feet spreading through the Temple. The bruised and sodden figures of the women lay everywhere.

For moments I watched the God bleeding. Then, overcome with the odor and the spectacle I stumbled out of the door into the garden. Now it has grown light and the army on the hills blows its trumpets and lies flattened on the rocks peering into the valley. From my room in Sebastien's house I can see them moving and the figures of Piltendorff leaping up and down in their midst. There is another figure that stands upright. At first it was strange to me but now I recognize Julian. He is beside Piltendorff and with him seems to be urging the figures to advance.

Sebastien has appeared. He is dressed in a black robe and sandals and carries a great sword in his hand. He is moving slowly across the valley toward the army on the hills. Alone and with the sword raised he advances. The army has risen to its feet. Led by Piltendorff and

Julian it is climbing over the rocks and entering the valley. Thousands upon thousands of figures are pouring down the hills, advancing upon Sebastien and his sword...

[18]

From the Journal of Mallare:—

Julian came into the room where I lay overcome by the thing I had witnessed. His face glowed and the smile I remembered him wearing long ago was on his lips. He stood regarding me silently until the suppressed elation I felt in his manner became unbearable.

"What do you want?" I cried.

"Health and freedom are the normal desires of man," he answered smiling. "These are still unachieved. Did you observe our victory or was the spectacle too improbable for you?"

"Where is Sebastien?" I asked.

"We have captured your redoubtable friend and thrown him into the Temple," Julian answered. "Ah, what a delightful battle. Did you admire our armies—our persistent, inexhaustible and heroic armies, Mallare?"

"Where did you find so many?" I watched them until I grew sick with their numbers."

"They were not found," he smiled. "Pilten-dorff and I made them. We sat for months, perhaps for years, fashioning mannikins that he and I could work by strings. They were all on little wheels and the General and I pulled them into the valley—thousands upon thousands of them. No sooner did Sebastien behead them than they sprang up again without heads. Hour after hour for three days he rushed among them swinging his sword. But there were too many. They were like a locust flight of warriors. They kept pouring over the hills down the rocks. Whichever way he turned he saw them, a grimacing and inexhaustible array moving continually upon him.

"On the second day he began to cry out. He stood with his eyes closed and his sword moving in a perpetual arc and roared in dismay as the avalanche of figures continued rushing down the hills. When you go out you will see. The valley is strewn with pieces of bark and paper and bits of wood—the results of your great hero's prowess.

"Finally on the third day dizzy with slaughter he fell to the ground and Piltendorff

and I who had been hard at work manipulating the puppets ran down the hill, pounced on him, bound him and carried him into the Temple. The grove was wet with blood. When we opened the Temple door a wave of blood higher than our knees rolled out. Synthemus is still bleeding. He stands with his head protruding from the Temple top, our arrow between his eyes and the blood runs out of his wound. We dropped Sebastien inside. He lies bound and helpless in a lake of blood surrounded by the corpses of his maenads."

I am left bewildered. How has this happened to Sebastien? He lies in the Temple, blood pouring slowly down on him. It is a trick. He has been fooled. He exhausted himself in a battle with shadows. I will go to him and untie his hands. Yet what are bonds to Sebastien? It is something else that holds him captive.

The days pass. Julian is busy in the streets. Aided by Piltendorff he runs about in pursuit of the hermaphrodites and the women who escaped that night. He binds them and with his shaggy companion carries them one by one into the Temple.

The island is becoming empty. Kora lies on a couch in the room below. Her eyes are closed and she seems to sleep. I stand beside her uncovered body. Beautiful and still, a faint breath moving behind the pallor of her skin, she lies on the couch where I found her first.

[19]

From the Journal of Mallare:—

An ominous air is over the Kingdom. I have no longer a desire to move. The valley is silent.

How hideous the Kingdom has become. The garden that circled the Temple has wilted. The huge flowers have collapsed and the earth is covered with dead blooms. The towers grow daily more formless. They melt like candles burning down and as they sink toward the earth they glitter with colors.

The Temple is dying. Its gigantic walls no longer fly into space. They bulge with decay. A collosal distortion overtakes them. Slowly as if under the blows of a mysterious calamity the Temple leans and its distant summit droops. I have waited for days for the debacle. Each moment promises to witness its crash across the island. Yet, wavering and drooping it continues to stand. The head of the God imprisoned in death still protrudes wearing the mammoth, withering flower as a collar.

As the tremendous stalk wilts, toppling into an ever deeper and more sinister arc, its walls blaze with a continual sunset. Phosphorescent seas appear to run down its broken sides. The flames and banners of decay creep out of its roots and spread in slow and ghostly conflagrations toward its summit. Daily the spectacle of its dissolution increases. Alkaline pinks and excremental yellows, purples and lavenders like tumerous shadows; browns that float like collosal postules through seas of lemon; reds that ferment into wavering islands of cerise and salmon, that erupt into ulcerous hills of scarlets and magentas—these revolve about the walls, mounting into vast patterns and dissolving one into the other. Slowly death postures in its coquettish shrouds.

But I no longer watch. Like a gigantic lamp the Kingdom sputters and expires. The stone hills move with carnelian shadows. The towers vanish in fanfares of color. The very earth swims in fulgurations. The veins of life burst and pour themselves out in a carnival of death. Spreading its plumage in a hallelujah of

ghostly flames, the Kingdom takes flight, its miracles blazing for a final moment and vanishing. Already darkness sits in its corners—a darkness out of which rise the odors that are the last gestures of life. These embittered farewells of matter foul the air until breathing becomes a horror. A stench comes from the shadows and spreads like an invisible and malignant corpse over the island. Rancid and suffocating it crawls out of the streets and towers and thickens into a fetid, overpowering mist around the withering Temple.

Julian entered the room where I sit waiting. He spoke to me in a gentle voice. A ship is being built. It will be ready soon. On it we will sail from the island. I listened without replying or raising my eyes to him.

It grows dark. There is no longer day or night but a yellow twilight through which the decaying valley blooms and reeks.

[20]

From the Journal of Mallare:—

Piltendorff has disappeared. Julian alone remains and Kora who still sleeps. I have been to the Temple and come back. It will fall soon. It has toppled almost to the ground. Its flower has rotted and dropped away. The entire island is covered with its dust. The head of the God hangs like an enormous pollen out of the Temple mouth.

As I approached it the odors like invisible sentinals guarding its collapse rushed upon me. Half blinded I stared at the tremendous ruin. I remembered its appaling symmetry, its roaring and vanishing walls. Now crippled and putrescent its enormity sprawls in the embrace of destruction. It crouches, barren and threatening against the sky.

I pushed through the sodden remains of the grove and came to the door. It fell away to

dust under my touch and covering my face
against the stench I stepped inside.

Ah, this soaring and radiant temple through
whose mysterious walls life once leaped in an
endless cataract. How vast and white it loomed
on the day its door opened to the God. It is
rotted now. Its dead walls hidden in ferrugin-
ous shadows murmur with the verminous hosts
that have spawned out of its decay. Its floor is
a crust of blood, thick and broken, out of which
the bodies of women protrude in gestures of
death. Masses of flesh fallen from the God lie
decomposing and covered with multitudes of insatiable, vulturous insects.

In the center, bent in a collosal bow, stands
the God rotted away to a blackened, reeking
cadaver. The vast bones of his body glisten
through the eaten spaces. Armies of white and
swollen maggots move like a continuous and fluttering shadow over this orgie of decay. The
monster, crusted with blood, its gigantic entrails
gleaming like phosphorescent walls, fills the
place with vile exhalations as if He still
breathed, as if the tattered and moulded flesh
over which the verminous feasters swarm with

an exultant hum, still throbbed with a dark and nauseous life.

For moments I stood as if I had fallen into some subterranean vat wherein the final rites of life celebrated a foul and blasphemous reveal. Veins of light opened through the gangrenous shadows around me. Amythist and sulphurous clouds bubbled out of the darkness. The maggots crackling like rain, buzzing like racing wheels raised a hideous chant of death. Frantically they overran each other, swelling into opaline clusters and falling in huge balls through the air. Puffed into beetle shapes, they rained from the feast and lay in a glittering and animate design over the crust of blood. But beyond these, beyond the ever fresh clouds of vermin hurling themselves upon the dark banquet were other mouths, fouler and invisible; mouths into which life emptied itself in a last steam of odors and eruptions. Ah, whose hungers were these, whose horrible breath was this that glimmered around me? What venemous and lustful thing battened upon these vanishing forms? What greedy and jealous hands were torturing the cadavers about me into this infinite and mysterious dismemberment as if intent upon removing the now useless secrets of life?

Answer me Sebastien, you whom I left haggard and struggling in the midst of this corruption. You whose eyes raised themselves defiant and burning out of this cauldron of decay, answer me, who lies in the dead Temple with you? What mysteries do the maggots chant as they swarm over you? What is this thing you created, that had only the shadow of life for its body? I will return to you again. I will wipe your lips clean of the filth that encrusts you. You will stand up and tell me, Sebastien, who it is that has sent a plague upon our phantoms, who entered our dream and flung his hunger into our Kingdom. They devour us. Mouths consume us. Come out of this hiding place, Sebastien, or we vanish...

Yes, I saw him in there buried amid the refuse. He raised his head as I called. The Temple began to move. Groaning and dropping huge fragments of mould, the walls slid toward the earth. I looked once more for Sebastien but he was gone. Foul things rained on the place he had been. I fled through the door, crying out in terror. Without looking back I continued to run, until the gloom and stench of the island paralyzed me.

It is come. See beyond the window where the vast shape of the Temple rocks in the shadows. It is falling. A roar fills the darkness. It breaks, it totters. Clouds of gleaming dust billow over the island. It is gone. Above its grave the night, vast and unoccupied, stands like a sudden tomb.

[21]

From the Journal of Mallare:—

Shapes move in the darkness. The white boat sails away. All become dust, dust in which shadows stir.

These are ghosts out of the caverns of thought. These are emanations that hurl themselves at the back of my eyes, that creep and halloo through the corridors of life seeking an entrance into the dream. Pale, behind windows they cannot break, kings and queens, monsters and demons—listen to them. Here is their Kingdom in the dark, turned to dust.

Their hands tear holes. Their eyes gleam in me. Hey—they ride on heavy shod horses through the labyrinths of my brain, shouting and waving their arms. Listen to their hooves pounding in my head. They gallop. No end to their ride. Figures bubble out of the dust behind the horses. The monstrous and hilarious cavalcade thunders and screams seeking the road into the Kingdom.

Let me pour magic into a pot. Smoke rises, butterfly lights and odors. These are incantations. Come out. Mallare still holds the Kingdom. Dust and odors, corpses and mists—a Mallare made of smoke crawls on his hands and knees among them. He says I am mad, this silent one staring at me. Weep, fool. You who destroyed the road into the valley, weep and wring your hands. I am a beggar waiting outside black doors. This cowering one, this slave choking with odors, sitting in a night of dead dreams— he is Mallare. They dance behind the doors. They ride and cry out, where is the way into the Kingdom. The roads rock under their feet. Lightnings crack the black skies. Ah, who is it weeping? I hear noises of sorrow. The fool weeps for the white ship that is gone. Wait— the doors will open. Here I am. Open, let me in. Let me lie under the flying hoofs of riders. Open, let me creep to the feet of the dancers. There is only dust around me. Darkness and weeping. Hey, let me in and I will show you the road, the hidden road, the road that bursts into the Kingdom...

[22]

In his room above the river front surrounded with hideous objects, with the dead bodies of animals and humans piled in the corners, Fantazius Mallare was found after an absence of seven years. Wasted and stiffened he was discovered crouching at the feet of a dead woman.